THE VIRTUES OF
THE SOLITARY BIRD

THE VIRTUES OF
THE SOLITARY BIRD

Juan Goytisolo

TRANSLATED BY HELEN LANE

SERPENT'S
TAIL

The publishers thank Kathy Acker, Mark Ainley, Martin Chalmers, John
Kraniauskas, Mike Hart, Bob Lumley, Enrico Palandri, Kate Pullinger, for their
advice and assistance.

Library of Congress Catalog Card Number: 90–64192

British Library Cataloguing in Publication Data
Goytisolo, Juan *1931–*
The virtues of the solitary bird.
I. Title II. Series
863.64[F]

ISBN 1–85242–175–4

First published as *Las virtudes del pájaro solitario* by
Editorial Seix Barral, Barcelona, 1988. Copyright © 1988 by Juan Goytisolo

The Spiritual Canticle comes from *The Collected Works of St John of the Cross*,
translated by Kieran Kavanaugh and Otilio Rodríguez, © 1979 by Washington
Province of Discalced Carmelites. ICS Publications, 2131 Lincoln Road N.E.
Washington, D.C. 2002.

This translation copyright © 1991 by Serpent's Tail

This edition first published 1991 by
Serpent's Tail, 4 Blackstock Mews, London N4

Typeset in 11/13pt Sabon by AKM Associates Ltd, London

Printed by
Hartnolls Limited of Bodmin, Cornwall

From the inner wine cellar
of my Beloved I drank
ST JOHN OF THE CROSS, *Spiritual Canticle*

a wine that intoxicated us
before the creation of the vineyard
IBN AL FARID, *Al Jamriya*

I

the apparition had materialized, had appeared to us, at the top
of the staircase on a day like the others, no different from the
others

(no, don't start asking me about dates, what does a misleadingly precise month, day, year mean at this point, after
what's happened?)

as we sauntered nonchalantly back and forth from the salon to
the dressing rooms, crossed the foyer next to the showers where
several still sprightly young things and older, more experienced
ones much the worse for wear were devoting themselves with
the same pleasure to the lustral rites and, leaning on the Lady's
counter or the shelf with the illustrated weeklies, we contemplated the couples on the side benches, the tables carefully set
out by the waiter, the lamps with translucent glass shades, each
with a twisted bronze foot, aligned like the fasces of lectors, the
proprietress of the place used to say on evoking its history, the
pomp and splendors of the imperial inauguration

(imperial, yes, imperial, don't be skeptical, Napoleon and
Eugénie did live, did reign, it was a great event attended in its
day by the cream of society)

step by step, carefully, because of the weight and bulkiness of
its footgear

(the giant clodhoppers or clogs of a peasant woman)

we saw its endlessly long legs appear, its incredible scarecrow
trousers belted about its ghostly silhouette of a puppet moved
by tiny invisible strings or wires

had it entered like everyone else through the arch of the carriage
gate, crossed the little courtyard with nineteenth-century
bathtubs ingeniously planted with perennials, proceeded
toward the staircase and its gas lamps of outworn majesty,
opened the door giving access to our ravaged and destroyed
kingdom, paid sixty-five francs to the blonde cashier who gave
out tickets, little individual bars of soap, shampoo, and other
beauty products and aids to bodily cleanliness?

it's no use asking questions after all this time, as though you'd like to relive the minutes preceding the blinding mushroom of Hiroshima or the burial of Pompeii or Herculaneum, there weren't any tape recorders or video cassettes, things like that, dearies, just happen, the way a brazen hussy loses her cherry! from the staircase, most likely a winding one because of its incredible height, had it spied first of all the broken scale on which years ago we apprehensively kept tabs on our figures, the foyer we crossed lazily or hopefully on our way to the black chamber or the wardrobe racks, then had the clogs cautiously placed themselves on the lower steps broadening the field of vision of the figure and, at the same time, that of the overawed spectators, a big loose tunic over its filiform extremities, pouches or petticoats with dozens of dolls, a floating lilac- and rose-colored cape in which its face was enveloped as in a flag? don't be anxious, it couldn't be seen yet, the whole thing happened with deadly slowness, its movements were viciously languid, perhaps beneath the veil or the tangled locks (the thick and discontinuous veil formed by its long tangled locks), it was now taking in the lounge, the seats to one side covered with worn red oilcloth, Second Empire gas lamps, wall paintings of Near Eastern landscapes, green hills, horsemen, silhouettes with burnooses and haiques, a spiky minaret of a mosque, a half moon white as snow, a scene full of atmosphere, nostalgically familiar to our spirited lovers for a day, composed, according to the Lady, by a great artist, a discreet regular of those baths devoted to the bliss and cleanliness of the body, before, long before we, even the most intrepid veterans among us, had become initiates of the rites and ceremonies of the temple, had sought the tenderness lying in wait in the pupils of the tiger, that luminous and brutal ecstatic escape from the suffocating squalor of our lives, paradise, a flaming and fleeting paradise like all the edens of the world

but don't interrupt me even if at first glance I lose my way, my discourse, for all its zigzags and sudden breaks, has a leading thread, I know at exactly what point I abandoned the

description, its clogs or clodhoppers on the last step of the
staircase, the head, its head that is to say, hidden not only by
the thick veil of long tangled locks but also by a huge broad-
brimmed hat, black as a bat's wing, stark black, sinister,
terrifying, a living statue of the Commendatore, a real specter
screams
nobody thought of screaming, literally freaked out by the
sudden intrusion, the brutal impact of the disjointed silhouette,
petrified I tell you at precisely the point we found ourselves
when it entered, the Lady as well, surprised at her usual post
behind the counter with her stylized makeup and abundant
mane of bright orange-colored hair, incapable too, despite her
stage presence and proverbial nimble tongue, of uttering one
word, a simple remark or sign of condemnation of that fateful
intrusion into her territory, hypnotized as all the rest of us were
by the clumsy weightiness of the enormous shoes, coarse
darkness of the legs, voluminous cape or shroud, pouch stuffed
with bunches of celluloid dolls, dark plaited locks, eyes lying in
wait in the underbrush, tutelary hat whose bat wings seemed to
summon forth imperiously the flight of a flock of crows
did it look at you? did it cast a covetous gaze at any of you in
particular?
how the devil could anybody know, the locks of hair covered
everything, but a person could intuit behind them the flashing
incandescence of eyes, their pupils penetrating and voracious,
expert at the art of catching from amid the thicket of veils a
glimpse of the components of the scene and its frozen actors,
not the slightest intake of breath or sign of breathing, I swear to
you, just silence, sheer silence, everything stopped dead by the
leaden movement of its footgear, those clogs planted at the
spot where the staircase ended, ready to turn right and left, to
proceed perhaps to the counter of the minibar where the Lady
contemplated her like a moth caught in the circle of an intense
summer light, obsessed, blinded, crepuscular, resigned with
Inca-like majesty to an inexorably fateful destiny, to an arrival

foreseen in her secret treatises on astrology concerning the plagues at the end of the millennium, a patient reading of divinatory signs of the disaster that cornered and abruptly caught its prey, how otherwise to explain her immobility and lack of reflexive defense mechanisms, the terrible helplessness of her expression as the ungainly and churlish Apparition took over her kingdom, capriciously proceeded to choose her victims, point her witch's index finger with equal likelihood at the veteran with spongy flesh enveloped in the toga of a senatress or at the novice in slippers and chlamys, vernal and overwhelmed by its presence?

we were trapped, my dears, we couldn't breathe or move, the one we had so greatly feared had passed from the ambit of our nightmares to embody that allegory of the bald woman sowing discord, black broad-brimmed hat, veiled face, cape with the loose folds of a shroud, filiform extremities, heavy, bulky clogs, of enormous gravitational force

had she begun to drop the dolls, as though sowing handfuls of seed in that condemned mansion?

no, not yet, her lap was bulging with little figures of human appearance, either naked or with a mere semblance of clothes, but that I can't guarantee you, because she hadn't started her trek yet, she contented herself with making the coals burn brighter, her pupils fine-honed in the blackness, treacherously delaying the instant of mercy or execution clearly dependent on sheer chance

the Lady?

yes, the first one, she had to hit quickly and with perfect accuracy the pillar supporting her kingdom so as to neutralize the force of the myth and prevent the slightest hint of resistance, the prophecies she herself had formulated had to be fulfilled to the very letter, the intruder who had burst into the solar cyclical calendar and abruptly ruined our lives demanded as the first priority the total destruction of the theogony that sustained the house, it was written that we must be present as helpless witnesses of her punishment and immolation

pale, very pale, her blood seemed to have suddenly taken refuge in the bright red tint of her hair, through her smooth ash-gray skin, as in one of those multicolored illustrations intended for medical students, there could be seen the complete anatomy of her body with its muscles close to the surface and deep down, its organs, its viscera, its skeleton, all diaphanous and superimposed, the heart with its auricles and ventricles, the twisting streamer of the intestines, the now uselessly complicated digestive tract from the buccal orifice to the precipice of the rectum

panting, suffocating, gasping like a fish out of water, a hapless gilled, medusan, gelatinous creature, slowly reduced before our eyes to the fiery splendor of her hair, her radiant wig of an amazon fed on the spongy absorption of blood of a flaccid and decomposed organism, a coelenterate flattened out on the floor with its scalp of bright red filaments, the shock of artificial hair of the Lady, her denture of perfect whiteness, the sole elements saved from the shipwreck, immune to the blows of the intruder's paw, the implacable execution of the sentence that demoralized us

what to do after such an atrocity except to remain cowering and quiet with our gaze riveted on the grotesque figure, to contract our sphincters and lips, to force ourselves to hide our terror knowing for certain, as we did, that we were at the mercy of the one in the huge broad-brimmed hat, face veiled, cape with the ruffles of a shroud, filiform extremities, heavy, bulky clogs, of enormous gravitational force

the destructive mechanism of our lives had been set in motion with a long, withered finger, like the ivory spindle of a spinning wheel, it pointed at venerable ones clad in togas and strong gladiators, flung its little human figures on the floor, witnessed impassibly the process of ruin that transmuted us into a soft, formless mass, impregnated with humors, above which there floated decimated documentation, locks of hair, dentures, glasses, stubborn bones, a sinister archive of identifying signs as in the films on the extermination camps shown in the twilight of the Nazi Valkyries

She, the long-legged one, finally turned on her soles, left the Berber salon of the Lady strewn with tufts of hair and remnants of worn fabric, entered the subterranean cavity of the ticket windows and the nocturnal chamber of our nuptials

(inside which, favored by the darkness, we had been blissfully happy, without a care in the world)

she proceeded to the fulgurant reduction of her prey without a scream of terror or request for aid from the latter, as though the inevitable, foretold vision of that beanpole of a woman had swept away the entire array of our forces, insects defenseless in the face of the pesticidal fumigation, guinea pigs suddenly irradiated, everything happened with fascinating punctuality, medulla and encephalic masses dissolved, secretions and lymph of watery consistency, convulsed little figures, burned to a crisp, Horror, with a capital H, as She, with her big shoes, voluminous cape and stark black broad-brimmed hat visited the inner courtyard of our intimate ablutions, the steam room of marvelous rejuvenating mist, the Sauna of Saunas, imperturbably sowing her seed, swiftly extending the fateful finger, setting old hands and novices alike on fire, capriciously granting amnesty to a lover, pursuing her macabre round with hieratic solemnity

ascending spiral staircase, thirty-three

(yes, thirty-three, I've counted them carefully!)

iron steps on which she noisily placed her clogs, her implacable eyes concealed in the recondite depths of their sockets, all of her a tangle, widow's veils, limp limbs, lap bulging with celluloid dolls, the screeching ugliness of scarecrows, bat-wing hat hovering with heraldic insolence

(excuse me, girls, if I appear to contradict myself, at times I saw her as a crow but on gaining altitude, as she ascended, her membranous wings were those of a vampire come directly from

one of those castles that in seeming defiance of gravity crown
the rugged peaks of Transylvania
her face appeared on the landing where we were in the habit of
gathering to chat with each other or spy from there on the
hustle and bustle of the corridor, an endless parade of peplums
and togas, free or occupied cells, the door slammed shut in the
face of envious rivals by a lover with a marriage tie to someone,
times, those, of mental and physical license, a space especially
conceived for bliss in which the mistress of the house never set
foot, as though, absorbed in the labors of superintending the
subsoil, she had lost interest in our pleasure-garden of delights,
informed of everything in reality by the chatter of the worst
gossips of the Numantian temper and air of the ones dressed in
togas, the undeniable stubbornness of a strapping fellow, the
commotion caused by the disquieting modesty of a vestal with
embroidered nylon panties, the Lady who was in on everything,
repository of our troubles and boudoir secrets until the bitter
fulfillment of the prophecies, the Mene, Mene, Tekel Upharsin
traced on the wall of that delightful Babelonia by a furtive,
treacherous hand
thus do the glories of the world pass!
where are the snows of yesteryear, meeting an end that was far
more fortunate than that of the proprietress, a little pool
scarcely bigger than the puddle of piss of a bitch in heat, melted
down to the marrow of her bones in less time than it takes a fly
to copulate, skin, tissues, viscera, skeleton, the one exception
being her bright red wig and her denture with the derisive smile
(pardon me, all of you, for giving way to my feelings, my
morbid insistence on this hallucinatory scene,
I go back to the other one, to the intruder lying spreadlegged at
the top of the staircase)
imagine the scene, a feverish diaspora, tight-assed exodus of the
ones dressed in togas, the mad scramble of the young ones, the
deceptive sigh of relief of those shut up in the prison cells, shrill
screams of it's come, it's come, our turn has come, she's melted

the brains and the foundations of the mistress, we can't do anything against her or her evil shadow, her gaze goes straight through a person and radiates a deadly wave, it only takes her seconds to make wrecks of us!

then movement and voices had ceased, those who were in the corridors tried to blend in with the ash-gray walls on seeing that the doors of the little cells were opening as though they had been sucked up and revealing people all by themselves or in couples huddled next to the bunks in that vain and pathetic attitude of those fleeing from a volcano, petrified forever beneath the rain of ashes and lava, alive, still alive, but already mute, impotent, exposed to the glacial look and enslaving proximity of the ugly bird, choice victims of that programmed devastation, sudden decomposition of our organisms into carrion, consumed one by one like insects beneath a solar ray powered by a monstrous magnifying glass, fried, liquified, melted down, without screams of terror or gestures of panic

(no, no, no, I'm not exaggerating

that's how I saw her, see her, awake or dreaming, every time her image assails me)

brutal, insensitive, hieratic, cruel to the innocent and helpless, surrounded by the halo of her tremendous power, the crude fear associated with her acronym, that feeling of fatality that overwhelmed us from the moment of her announced visit and led to the resigned attitude of animals on their way to the slaughterhouse

the dazzling brightness of the great information machine had insidiously predisposed us to conformity and demoralization, nobody thought at the time of remedies or cures, the plague had attacked us like a falcon in a fierce and dizzying dive, life was a game of Russian roulette, we didn't know if the long-legged one with the hat and the veils would point at us with her finger or grant us a reprieve of months or weeks, panic destroyed our favorite haunts now slowly dying for lack of clientele and abandoned them to a spectral emptiness, closed by municipal

order or repeated threats, rusty padlock, ominous death notice
or announcement of a change of ownership on the door
(my imagination often recreates the abolished space, steam
bath and pool without a drop of water, salon with paintings on
the wall empty, corridors flecked with dusty sunlight, little
cells with inactive bunks, solitude of rooms once beatific and
now condemned)
the sower of discord has used up her supply of celluloid dolls
and observed in silence the havoc of her visit, residues of white
fungoid consistency or else melted, accumulation of wigs and
dental prostheses, little puddles still steaming, waste products
of incredible organic origin, the images of death and destruction seemed to reinvigorate her, her look, figure, dis-
proportionate members, cape, tangled locks, hat were precisely
those of the perverse heroine of the painting
(how the devil, I wonder, had the artist been able to intuit her
bursting in on the scene from a distance of almost eighty years?)
she seemed satisfied with her work all of a sudden
(at least that was how we interpreted her sour, strident smile)
she returned, feet backward, again stretched out her long legs
weighted down by the thickness and heaviness of her footgear,
flexibly adapted her silhouette to the spirals of the staircase,
traversed sauna and pool with the air of being the owner of the
place, nosed about the apocalypse of the black chamber, took
great delight at the spectacle of the salon, withdrew from the
ruins of eden with the same cold disdain with which she had
made her way inside
(was the blonde still sitting in her place at the ticket window?)
nobody ever found out whether she paid the set price it cost to
get in, exactly sixty-five francs

the hours, the days, the weeks in the garden, absorbed in endless, Boccaccian converse, minute reconstruction of events and adventures, instants of happiness and splendor, of spirited suppressed aggressiveness, realities or fantasies revealed with that painstaking care and desire for perfection of detail that exile dictates, scrupulous fidelity to the rites of the world that had disappeared, hands of the dial stopped at an unlucky date

spared from the catastrophe or plague, settled comfortably in their deck chairs and shell-shaped wicker chairs, forming a circle around the table with the tray of drinks, on the vast seaside terrace with its moss-covered balustrade and large pots of hydrangeas, a calm, warm late afternoon without the occasional relief of a breeze

fans, sighs, whispered words, a group of highborn ladies waging a quiet war against time and its avarice, perfidy, inconstancy, an interrupted trajectory full of snares, pauses of false bliss, like bees offering libations of memories in the contemplative peace of their tiny cells, still incredulous at the havoc of the ugly bird's cruel visit, that summer serpent, they had said at the beginning, invented by newspaper reporters

dressed with the somnambulistic elegance that the scene required, arborescent hats, feather boas, plumes like those of the far-distant vanished mansion, immobilized as well in the splendid illusion of late afternoon, the apotheosis of pastel pink tones in the background of the tableau we were staging, each one reciting or miming her own role in the drama, the evocation of past glories in the Lady's closed domains, the world forever divided in two, before and after the condemnation, the searing rain of ashes and lava

we were not able to leave that precisely bounded space, the fiction of a pleasure-garden with chairs, pots of hydrangeas and sea views, the compensatory dream of a hotel with the air of a beach resort, obliged to maintain the appearances of dignity and nobility forced upon us by misfortune, everything was a façade and we knew it, the liquid languished in the glasses, nobody took the tray away or brought more ice cubes, no waiter appeared to cast a watchful eye on the terrace

we had sensibly given up making any sort of request, clapping our palms together or ringing the disconnected call bell, we lived amid the vacuum of a bell jar, once past curtains, stage flats and papier-mâché walls there was an unknown territory infested with dangers, we clung like novice actresses to the text of the daily performance, stories of amorous dalliances in the Lady's house, nostalgic references to a good-looking lover, punctilious reliving in our memories of our peaceful days

(how was it possible that the sun prolonged its fire indefinitely, that the clouds did not change their pleasing rosiness and a bird silhouetted with innocent gracefulness hovered for hours without even moving its wings?)

we were terrified at the thought of leaving the place, transgressing the limits of our theater and confronting the brutality of what was happening, speeches filtered through the suspended scenery and flies above the stage, elementary counsels of prudence broadcast in muffled tones by loud-speakers, radio or tv messages, announcements of draconian measures concerning hygiene, strict prohibitions against the consumption of vegetables and milk, orders to put weather stripping around the doors and windows, to remain inside our dwellings, to scrub the floors carefully, to shake and brush dresses and other apparel exposed to the dust and contamination of the irradiated air

gutteral, threatening voices that aggravated the awareness of our exile, added questions and uncertainties to the already overwhelming sensation of precariousness, what was happening outside seemed to respond like an echo to the inner devastation that assailed us, increased our sense of being hemmed in and under siege, subjected us to that illusory stage whose audience was ourselves, endless repetition of soliloquies and litanies, stories and more stories aimed at keeping the silence in check

(no, we were not on the terrace of a hotel, the doors and windows that apparently communicated with the salons and dining rooms had been cleverly painted in so as to sustain our illusion, the whole thing was a cardboard theater set, the round red sun, the clouds that turned pink in the late afternoon, the large pots of hydrangeas, the deck chairs)

condemned to talk so as to extend the run of our performance, to make hollow gestures and assume empty expressions, to fan ourselves delicately, to raise to our lips an already drained glass on the tray of drinks, to go into ecstasies over the apocryphal quiet of the twilight, to rush to the lookout point represented by the balustrade and watch from there, with feigned interest, the motionless, unreal, make-believe sea

(when would the fishermen arrive, someone sighed, though there were no fishing boats in sight)

inane gestures and phrases whose object was to add a touch of perfection to the scene, vying with each other in raising the tone of our voices, accentuating the dark circumflex of our eyebrows, curving our bejeweled little finger with the stiffness of a rooster's spur, emphatically opening our fans like beauties in mantillas in the first row at the bullring, finally drowning out with our coquettish hysteria the obsessive drone of the loudspeakers that besieged us, evacuation orders, curfew, ominous references to the epidemic, radioactive isotopes, iodine 131, thyroid saturation, gamma rays

were we living between parentheses once again, granted a temporary amnesty or was it the beginning of a vague new aggression like the one that had turned us into ghosts? none of us knew or wanted to know, chiromanceresses and divineresses had died, nobody dared consult horoscopes, we were living, we were nourishing ourselves on the past alone, a return to our luminous days, adorned and embellished by memory, a fleeting exhumation of banal or amusing happenings, her own version of which each one tried her best to impose, so as to assume an imaginary leading role

and then the quarrels

the no, no that wasn't how it was, I was there, I saw the whole thing, things didn't happen the way you tell them, you were in the banquettes at the back with your lover and she, the Seminarian, came in like this, take a good look at me, because I can reproduce every last one of her gestures exactly, with the towel wound round her head like a turban, thrusting her ugly hyena's mug forward with a provocative air, eyes ringed with a nimbus of kohl, hands on her hips, she looked as though she were about to devour the world, steal the other one's fiancé, scratch her with her fingernails like a common whore, but nobody looked any more because it was the hundredth repetition of the squabble and we didn't feel we had the strength to cut her short, better to leave her to her number as, tired now of studying our faces and attire in our little mirrors, we stood up to stretch our legs, flatten our noses against the painted doors and windows, dejectedly contemplate balustrade and pots of hydrangeas, the cheery backdrop of late afternoon with the fake sun as plump as an orange in the clouds

there was no way out, we were caught in the net and the increasing volume of the loudspeakers confirmed the relent lessness of the siege, covered the forced animation of the talk with the slow ebb and flow of the tide

were they trying to intimidate us in this way, to guide us back to the fold like sheep gone astray, to force upon us a behavior conforming to the glacial geometry of their programs?

the refuge we had thought we would find in the garden, in the peace of a few weeks in the garden, devoted like fugitives of centuries past to the cultivation of the arts of Scheherazade had turned out to be a fallacy, our presence in that place was that of actresses of an unwritten work obliged to improvise on the stage set of a terrace with views of the sea what an invisible audience expected of them, not knowing whether this audience really existed or was simply obeying the whims of the

mysterious inventor of the scene
a god, a crazy, a demiurge, a poet?
was there a possibility of rebelling, taking the sun down from
the backdrop, overturning the drink tray with the empty
glasses, challenging the authority of the threatening loudspeakers?
none of us was sure, we were just barely existing, confused and
depressed, we clung to any false rumor or sheet anchor, the
sudden invasion by the Lady with the one-syllable name had
given us the final blow, we were living on or dying on, the
reprieve was a sort of ritual sentence whereby through putting
up with our theater we were learning to interiorize the disgust
and contempt of the others, their immutable hatred for
everything we embodied
stopping or going on: what difference did it make?
outside, the loudspeakers wailed on.

she had gone out with the intention of taking a breathing spell, getting a bit of fresh air, walking along the old streets of the district of the city next to the docks where we used to relax before the silent explosion of that bomb whose shock wave decimated the population but respected with canny foresight the integrity of the buildings

something thought up by an absolute genius, as had been explained to us by Neutrona, a graduate of M. I. T. from some years back, destroying people's organic defenses but leaving intact the sacred principles of private property

(genius which, in all truth, had been of no use to her, since Neutrona, like all those of the select group of our scientists, had been pushing up daisies in New Calvary or Mount Olivet for months now)

but to return to my own story

to that no doubt rash decision to leave her hiding place so as to find out something about the others in their community, to learn of their fate and vicissitudes, how many were still alive or had died, exchange news, be up on what was going on, listen to reasonable advice and words of consolation

she had provided herself (I had provided myself?) beforehand with a lilac-colored organdy dress with lace ruffles and big bows, bead necklaces, medals and cameos, white stockings, high-heeled pumps with rhinestone buckles at the instep

made up like a mask, stylized eyebrows and eyelashes, mascara, rouge, rice powders, flaming scarlet heart-shaped lips

hat of arborescent structure with ramifications, flowers and fruit, artistically adorned with little birds and plumes, marvelous, disturbing and unreal in its sophisticated and corrupt beauty

in a city such as this, she said to herself, nothing better than to adopt brazen and provocative airs so as to obtain the gift of passing unnoticed

but was she her or me?

for I see myself, I see her, from inside and outside, with the makeup, dress and hat, warily appearing at the door of the modest two-story brownstone, tottering on the way downstairs as though negotiating the mainstay of a ship tossed by a violent tempest

the neighborhood had a hostile and phantasmagorial air, living quarters locked and bolted, buildings and shops closed by the health authorities or neighborhood self-defense associations, threats and accusations spray-painted on the walls

THOSE INFECTED CLEAR OUT
A SICK ONE LIVES HERE
THE ONE ON THE FIFTH FLOOR
HAS A FEVER AND THROWS UP

our dens and lairs of bliss had been pillaged, subjected to the fire that purifies, reduced to a twisted skeleton of charred ruins and an acrid, stubborn, clinging odor, of disinfectant or burned flesh, lingered in the streets and the deserted areas near the piers and docks abandoned decades before by the transatlantic steamship lines

I walked along enveloped, half blended into a poisonous fog like the one that emanates from the swamplands of Louisiana in the early hours of the morning, my footsteps were those of a sleepwalker, despite my careful appliance of makeup my face was beaded with sweat and I wiped it away from beneath the transparent veils of my hat with a little embroidered handkerchief, my figure stood out against the blue background of the melancholy crepuscular fog, I felt incapable of reacting urgently to the gravity of the danger that threatened, the patrolling of the streets by local residents on the lookout for those who were plague-ridden, what to do except to lean weakly against a lamp post, hidden in the cloud of steam rising from the ground and making the outline of objects unreal?, a brief closeup of my eyes eloquently summed up my anxiety, would I, poor thing, be able to stand up to such a test? would I be capable of drawing strength from my visible and heartrending weakness?, the passersby whose path I crossed

covered their mouths with their hands or condemned me with
an inquisitorial movement of their fingers, no one took pity on
my faded splendor or offered me words of encouragement, they
went swiftly on their way with hatred and fear painted on their
faces, the spectacle of my vulnerability incited their rancor and
their rage, they were perhaps readying themselves to denounce
my presence to the others, to hunt down the authors of the
sacking and burning, I should have retraced my steps and
gotten myself out of danger without wasting a moment but
fatalism, anxiety, the heat immobilized me, I wanted to get
away and couldn't, my body did not obey my will, its
movements were slow and sluggish, a fascination similar to
that of prey trapped in the slavering filaments patiently
secreted by a spider kept me inert and chloroformed, the voices,
the barking, the orders grew more violent still, the evil-tongued
informers had fulfilled their function and the pack was coming
to catch its victim in the dead-end streets of the neighborhood,
my pursuers, as I could see, were wearing rubber gloves and
gauze masks as a precaution against contagion, I was fleeing
from them in the teeth of the furious wind whipping the
feathers and the veils of my hat and I could hear, closer and
closer, their shouts, exclamations, panting breath, what were
they going to do to me?, put me in a cage?, exhibit me in the
streets like a trophy?, finish me off with a burst of their
pesticides?, hermetic faces, oxidized by the corrosive salt air
passed me by one after the other like an endless traveling shot,
everything contributed to making the race an unequal one,
putting obstacles in my path, the stiletto heels of my pumps got
twisted, I had lost my sense of direction and didn't even know
where my footsteps were taking me
what you're telling you saw in a film, I said to myself
was that true?
dignified, every inch the lady, offended, I broke off the story

the hunters turned up one fine day with their nets and methodically combed the trees, hedges and thickets of avenues and parks where we used to rendezvous, the tall ficus, magnolias and flame trees in whose shadow we commented on the events that shook our little kingdom and the threats that weighed heavily upon it, awaited the desired partner like turtledoves, freely showed our plumes or modulated our little trills with growing apprehension

then, when their hunt became a matter of common knowledge and we crouched prudently in our nests, they resorted to the old trick of the baited trap to catch us, the rumor cleverly started by some infiltrator and then repeated by boobies and little lovebirds, that they were going to regularize our situation and allow us to leave, the lure of a new school of the dance for persons of artistic sensibility or a fondness for ice skating, even the incredible story of a visit by the Grand Duchess Anastasia, we were taken prisoner by the hundreds in the place where we had been invited to assemble, happy as larks and completely taken in by their vicious lies

(the gardens and public promenades lulled in bygone days by soaring and warbling offered a desolate picture of stillness and silence, nobody moved in the branches any more or raised their voices in song, the entire city seemed like a cardboard stage set as did the confounded seaside resort we were locked up in)

they had herded us together in the sports stadium, like in the old films about the Vel d'Hiv that had made us shed so many tears years before, so as to line us up for rollcall, make a police file on us, group us in production units, load us into trucks like cattle, cross interminable dusty plains, savannas, tundras, taigas of desolating pleonastic repetition, piled one atop the other, parched with thirst and hysterical, as acrimonious and aggressive as a nest of scorpions, the loudspeakers broadcast slogans mobilizing us against the old social vices, the guards proved to be implacable, we were doomed to disappear like birds of an extinct species, to give way to the youthful

dynamism that these others embodied, three days and nights of
cold and heat without a wink of sleep because of the din of
their everlasting propaganda speeches till we were herded on
arrival at our destination into smelly barracks amid orders,
shouts, whistles, dogs, watchtowers, barbed wire, a scene of
overwhelming depression from which we escaped as best we
could whenever the marquise and her notables visited us
we had invented a choreography for *Swan Lake* whose
rhythms, movements and tableaux we knew by heart because
we had practiced them among ourselves before the roundup, a
number of us mimed it almost to perfection, look at me, all of
you, listen, this way, exactly this way, imitating the prima
ballerina in her winged leaps and graceful gestures, that
exquisite grace amid the wasteland comforted us, we felt
ourselves levitate in our leotards and tutus, achieve the sinuous
elegance of the swan, revive the evanescent agony which in the
theater brought tears to our eyes, to cover up what we were
doing we went on working with our hateful tools, one with a
pick, another with a hoe, a third with a shovel, the previously
announced or impromptu arrival of the marquise galvanized
us, the guards' agitation and their running this way and that,
the hurried orders to clean up and decorate the camp in which
they held their meetings and commemorative services indicated
that the retinue had left the castle and was approaching our
farm, come on, get a move on, the officer screamed at the top of
her lungs, cussing all of us out and losing her cool altogether,
repaint me the shields, watchwords and emblems, the
Liberator's bust and base, everything must be clean as a
whistle, shine like a communion plate, did you all hear, I'm
going to put the ones that goof off or goldbrick on bread and
water in their cells, only work can redeem you and restore your
dignity you bitches, as we pretended to obey and vied with each
other in performing this pantomime, this chorale of lady
tractor drivers or women workers with imperturbable smiles,
heroines of an ideology shown in color illustrations in the pages

of our magazines amid a sea of waving grain with all the tender edifying details fondly worked out by the artist, awaiting the moment when the guards assigned lookout duty on the hilltop would give the word and present arms, unleash a whirlwind of insults, bugle calls, orders barked out in plain words and we would see the landaus and carriages of the retinue appear on the horizon, the marquise's black tilbury with her footman dressed as a marschallin, an apparition, I swear to you, whose aura of exoticism tore us away from the ideal setting of the swans, from the subtle lightness of the dance, like parrots trained in the rites of her doctrine, we began the swift Stakhanovite simulacrum with cheerful countenances, full of assurance and optimism in our impetuous storming of the goals, the conquest and exploitation of those remote and fertile lands, the marquise contemplated us through her field glasses and we danced a pas de deux for her, we allowed ourselves to be carried away by the music, we refined even further the agility and clarity of the movements, it did not matter at all to us that in the fervor of the enterprise we had dropped our supposed work tools, the death throes of the swan exalted us and we acted without ulterior motives, we aspired only to attain the concise lightness of her fluttering wings, the ethereal equilibrium of steps en pointe, that ineffable expression of languor at the cruel instant of her decline, the boots and uniforms had been transmuted into the tutus and gauze skirts of ballerinas, our profiles were silhouetted with exquisite delicacy and the audience awaited the fall of the curtain to burst into tumultuous applause

old, exhausted, sweaty, we did our best to whirl like drunken tops, we leapt with the awkwardness and short flights of barnyard fowl, the music we dreamed of existed only in our heads, the Nijinsky-like entrechats were mere clumsy imitations and we barely remained en pointe in precarious equilibrium, ostriches rather, broad in the beam and plucked clean, something frightful, take my word for it, the women officers said nothing and copped out, but the marquise didn't care for our show, it was plain to see that the whole thing didn't appeal to her, and she, ordinarily so talkative and such a show-off, just sat there in the coachman's seat of the tilbury, inscrutable, distant, withdrawn, inspecting us with neither kindliness nor tender affection, through the smoke of her cigar

I'd call that jumping from the frying pan into the fire, from the domain of a marquise owning lives and landed property into the hands of someone who never announces her visit, the accursed, grotesque, one-syllable figure who keeps us confined here

she had gotten up from the table after lighting a Philippine cigarette in her long amber holder and was pretending to settle down comfortably on the balustrade, absorbed in the contemplation of the seascape, still without a breeze having come up, since there's no end to this dead calm they're going to have to postpone the yacht races, a remark that prompted the usual conversation concerning the weather, the exhausting afternoon without a sign of its ever ending, the waiter's inexplicable delay in bringing more drinks, the suspect immobility of the hydrangeas planted in the big pots, they don't even take the trouble to water them, they'll soon wilt in all this heat

no one was talking now about ringing the call bell or complaining to the management of the resort, any hope of seeing the staff appear had vanished, there seemed to be very few guests for that time of year and there was no movement visible through the doors and windows that opened onto the terrace from the dining room and the salons

had they suddenly fled from the place on discovering the magnitude of the disaster?

beyond the space marked off by the overhead flies and suspended stage sets, the loudspeakers went on with their interminable explanations of the rules of hygiene and preventive measures, warning against panic, announcing plans for a general evacuation in case of danger, a liter of milk contains 720 becquerels one of the guests had said, the most important thing of all is to brush yourselves off but, once the first phase of confusion and alarm was over, when some of us had complained of nausea and headaches, we showed no sort of skin rash or any other clinical symptoms, our artificial redoubt had been mysteriously exempted if we could at least hear a foreign radio broadcast, here everything is subject to censorship, they radiate you one fine day with two hundred thousand millirads and you don't have the least idea, so to speak, how long it will be before you kick the bucket!

but, how to get a radio without going beyond the limits of the terrace, that hermetic and asphyxiating space in which we naïvely felt safe?

then the one in the corner, decked out like a lamp with a fringed shade and tassels and fluting, began to cry out, overcome with one of her habitual attacks of hysteria, come on, tell us, open your trap, something that happened to you or something you saw, mortal agony, a death, the hideous end of the Seminarian!

and they all suddenly started talking, gesturing, making faces, their hips and shoulders swaying, the Seminarian encapsulated in her hermetic cell, separated from the other sick ones, stewing in her own slime, a grotesque sight straight out of a horror show, emaciated, covered with buboes, all nails and hair, she scratched furiously at the walls of her bubble, trying to get out and contaminate the air we breathed, the doctors had put a cross on her charts and nobody was even taking care of her now, just one nurse dressed in a space suit served meals to her through a hole

tell us, tell us!

we saw her decompose little by little like a fungous pap, finally they fed her intravenously and her body, what was left of her body, was connected to dozens of little plastic tubes, the bloody bitch clung to life like a leech and we asked the nurse to prolong it so as to enjoy the spectacle, wearing our little masks and half dead with laughter, we went right up close to her, to get a good look at her, more viscous and dehydrated each time

was she suffering?

yes, of course she was, she was writhing in pain, the

tranquilizers and drugs were of no help at all
did she cry out?
the glass walls let no sound through, just the sight of her
contractions and spasms
and the one with the Philippine cigarette holder went out onto
the apron of the stage and mimed the scene for the audience,
constructed the bubble that isolated the Seminarian with
precise, graphic gestures, sharply outlined, oval, transparent,
an inviolable chalk circle traced with the wisdom of a sorceress,
each movement of her hands served as evidence to us of the
strict nodular nature of the separation, the diaphanous
sphericity of the prison in which the poisonous creature gasped
for breath, the magic rite delighted the spectators, they spurred
her on with their shouts to continue her number, the viperess
was getting the punishment she deserved, the daily depiction of
her death agony made them forget their misfortunes, go ahead,
they urged her on, multiply her buboes, swell her medusa-face,
reduce it to a mass of gelatine, we want to see how she
explodes!
till the exhaustion from the pantomiming, repeated day after
day, left all of us empty and drained, sitting once more like a
group of highborn ladies around the cocktail table, absorbed in
the contemplation of that perpetual afternoon whose fiction lit
in mocking rose tints the barren décor of the terrace

seated with a certain rigidity as if awaiting the artist who
would immortalize them in a portrait, they had meanwhile
changed their costumes and accessories, they now displayed
themselves with greater solemnity and sumptuousness, umbelliform or bell-shaped tutelary hats, ostrich-feather plumes,
monocles held tensely in place over an insolent blue eye, folding
pearl-handled opera glasses, immense flabella that closed and
opened to fan themselves with the ostentatious adroitness and
swift disdain of offended royal peacocks

the décor of the place had also changed, minor modifications
trivial enough at first sight but whose novelty introduced a
note of relief in that atmosphere of anxiety charged with
repressed tensions, someone had removed for example the tray
with the empty glasses which allowed one to presuppose the
subsequent arrival of the waiter with a fresh round of drinks,
the painted hydrangeas in the simulated pots lent the terrace a
less gloomy air inasmuch as they had been replaced by careful
plastic reproductions of shrubs with green leaves and pink
petals, even the solar sphere painted above the seascape of the
backdrop on which the balustrade figured in the foreground
appeared less fiery and beaming than usual and gave the
impression of having gone backwards in its orbit of descent as
though someone had turned the hands of time counter-
clockwise

how marvelous, one of them remarked, the days are going by in
reverse, we're getting younger instead of older and leaving a
whole bunch of years behind, the hypothesis had thrilled us, we
were there in hibernation, removed from the round of the
seasons and its insatiable hunger for human lives, larval, unable
to sleep, enthralled, bathed in a diffuse and perpetual summer
light similar to that of the Arctic plains, our refuge was in truth
a privilege, by fleeing from the plague we were also escaping the
inexorable rigor of time, we were living the potential condition
of chrysalises, isolated in that remote spa extremely difficult to
locate we were renewing ourselves without surgical operations

or Rumanian hormone treatments, our world would rise from the ashes like the phoenix and restore to us once again, listen to me, life's savor, the lustral rites and the corporeal glory of the Turkish baths, restored temple of love, tabernacle of flaming, transparent glass, Sauna of Saunas, a great ceremony of remembrance and expiation, purification of the place with the burning of aromatic herbs and incantations, exorcisms sung in tenor and soprano voices, a cortège of lovers and novices with lighted tapers, come on, this minute, everybody line up, perfect your gestures of piety, refine to the limit of the sublime your seraphic poses, we must transmit urbi et orbi the most serene loftiness of our message, humbly obeying the orders of the Archimandrite with her amber cigarette holder arrayed with all the pomp that the circumstances demanded, cope, miter, ring, crosier, solemn, hieratic, assisted by deacons and altar boys in snow-white tunics, prayers, offerings and vows to the Virgin, an ailing and anemic nymphet borne on a portable platform, beat of drums, clouds of incense, resurrected royal purples, rain of roses, slow advance, rhythmical step, gradual convergence of the confraternities of penitents in the imperial salon of the Lady, red banquettes, wall paintings with a Near Eastern theme, gas lights of an anachronistic luxury, mirrors in which we saw reflected the hope and dream of future and past marriage ties to our lovers, receptacle now of the prayers of contrition and sorrow intoned in falsetto by the Archimandrite and repeated by the cortège with gestures and grimaces of compunction, Madre mía amantíssima, in every moment of life, be mindful of me, a miserable sinner, a masculine termination whose incongruity we did not even notice, transfigured by the zenithal light of the great stained glass window that in former times sheltered our courting, gathered together in the salon as in the good old days, observing a minute of touched silence before the counter of the minibar on which the proprietress fell, struck down by a lightning blow, a cruel memory, a piercingly painful evocation that brought tears to our eyes and plunged us once again into the nightmare of the grotesque figure, the sudden apparition of the ungainly one in the hat on the stairs with her cruel store of seeds for sowing discord

had she been vanquished meanwhile by science, exorcised by religion, plunged into Pluto's domains in just retribution for her horrible deeds?

the situation was unreal but we felt comforted, the pomp of the procession, the prayers and invocations of the Archimandrite inordinately proud of her Latin, the echo of the antiphonies and Deo gratias restored to those rooms long closed their exuberant and festive air, the ones clad as deacons and altar boys had purged the racks of the cloakroom and the black chamber with their censers, opened the door of the showers next to the pool and the steam rooms and a subtle breath of amorous scenes and aquatic exploits touched the penitents' voices grown gradually more and more languid, lessened the sincerity of their sighs and the beating of their breasts in contrition, precipitated an insidious modulation of the s's of the Madre mía amantíssima, transmuted the Archimandrite into a resplendent opera diva, heavily made up, opulent, magnificent, cope with feathered edges, miter with the plumes of a cuirassier, crosier turned into a scepter, pastoral ring held out for the candid kiss of the novices or the insolent gliding tongue of the senatresses in togas, on her way already, with her pages, attendants, buffoons and ladies in waiting to the spiral staircase traversed in days of yore by the assiduous offerers of libations of pollen eager to fulfill their devotions on the modest kneeling stools of the roomettes, flabby and lustful, lifting the lower edges of her cope to show her contempt, revealing, with cunning coquetry, the high-heeled shoes and purple stockings, adapted, like the garter belt and panties, to the penitential nature of the ceremony that she was presiding over, exorcism of the plague and homage to its victims, driving away evil spirits with clouds of incense, joyful restitution of those chambers to their original purpose, imperial inauguration evoked by the Lady amid sighs in those black months, full of rumors and presentiments, which preceded the arrival of the grotesque figure, a nuptial temple for us and the lovers we encouraged, who shower us with attentions, a destiny recovered intact, amid fervent Te Deums, by those of us who had been saved after so many trials and tribulations

from the place in which I found myself, if I was at any precise point on the staircase and not floating capriciously like gossamer as it appears to me in retrospect, what most attracted my attention was the posterior opulence of the Archimandrite, her behind with immense buttocks uncovered at each step by the bold flight of the cope, the plump, hairy calves, the thighs bulging beneath the flowers of the garter belt and purple lace hose, young ladies in waiting and pages helped her climb the stairs and fanned her gluttonous poop with childish impishness, come on, girls, sing, she panted, your angelic voices should resound in this tabernacle of happiness, novices first and then the veterans, the Pange lingua everybody, on fire, inflammatory, eager to reach the floor above and make certain that armed lovers were keeping a close eye on the doors of the cells, invested with the licentious majesty of her attire, waggling her hips and shoulders, throwing kisses at those about to tie the connubial knot, a Philippine cigarette in the beak of the thin amber holder, the lustra sex and membra panis of the hymn intermingled with salacious winks, rapid circular movements of her tongue, benedictions with the crosier topped by a grotesque phallus, exultant and insolent in her movements of an old rumba dancer as thudding, stamping boot steps echoed louder on the staircase, came up, drew nearer, sowed terror, routed us helter-skelter, papier-mâché doors and windows seemed to be shaken by a hurricane, the loudspeakers thundered in an unknown language, the stage set of the balustrade with its sunset and pots of hydrangeas was brusquely hauled up into the flies of the theater and we discovered that we were surrounded by a crowd of nurses wearing gauze masks

they're Kirghiz women! the Archimandrite had cried out in horror

explosion, accident or radioactive leak, what was certain was that fatal doses of cesium, iodine, ruthenium and strontium were contaminating the air we were breathing, it was imperative to follow instructions carefully, take the pills they offered us, prepare to travel, evacuate that deceptive refuge, rush to the point where trucks were waiting for us before the cloud covered the area and we were pitilessly swept away

grass, little flowers, bees, sweet summer solicitude, solar
benevolence, soft breeze, gentle conjoining of hills, fertile
countryside, tinkle of little bells, echo of ax blows, syncopated
voices, faint barking of dogs, serene verdure of promenades
lined with poplars and riverbank foliage

they occupy a dozen wicker chairs with imposing backs, kings
and queens on their thrones with heraldic emblems, but you are
unable to determine clearly if you are with them or see them
from outside the scene, lying in ambush in another place in the
meadow

nor do you recognize their figures at all or manage to identify
them, they frequently change position and appearance, the
well-groomed blonde on the left suddenly sits down to rest on
one of the chairs in the center yet her fungiform hat covers the
head of the gentleman in glasses just settled down in his
armchair

as in one of those cardboard settings at fairs with holes through
which customers wanting to have their pictures taken as
bullfighters, flashily dressed hustlers, soccer players or NASA
astronauts joyfully poke their heads, satisfied with the exotic
personality that such attire gives them, you discover that
whereas the outfits remain exactly the same the faces change
despite the disorienting frequency of their movements, the
enduring family air of their physiognomies begins to intrigue
you

couldn't that withered, angular face of the lady with the stole
and hat be that of Doña Urraca, the widow of the glorious
martyr to the cause and the adoptive godmother of a youngster
in the trenches? doesn't the man with the hair cropped so close
to his skull that it looks shaved and a more or less simian air
about him remind you, despite the leggings and the tight-
fitting jacket, of the flamboyant Don Blas of your childhood,
with his showy chaplain's cape and bulletproof religious image
over his heart?

the new civil dress, of punctilious, elegance, superimposes

without in any way effacing it, on the previous image, remote now, of his conversations in your uncles' garden, they too seated in wicker armchairs in the arbor, in the shade of the acacias

the war is over and your side is governing the country!

the doctor, the nurses, Don Blas, Doña Urraca are perhaps brushing away the dust from faded memories, stale and moldy episodes, hoary and eroded exploits without being aware of your presence in the vicinity, unrecognizable no doubt after all this time

with binoculars you also contemplate the quiet retreat in which half a dozen burly bruisers with oiled bodies and rough leather shorts are engrossed in their virile games, prolonging the sweet and vinelike embrace, lifting each other into the air, gliding about with the suppleness of snakes, enveloping each other with straining muscles, seeming to copulate and devour each other

the beauty of the scene overwhelms you with joy and you would like to draw closer to the contenders, breathe in the fierce aroma of their oil, absorb yourself in the sinuous union of the prey, admire their bodily texture, obtain the grace of a smile from them

the characters seated in a semicircle attempt to dissuade you with gestures indicative of danger but you will pay no attention to them and continue on your way to the glory of your feather-mattress nuptial arena bathed in the fecundating luminosity of the day

the subtle and colorless bird, silhouetted with innocent gracefulness in the sky, appears to fly and yet remain immobile, suspended with gravity-free litheness above the grass mat on which the smiling wrestlers lie waiting

II

all that, said the other, corresponded approximately to my psychosomatic reactions during the various phases of the treatment, the sleep cure prescribed by the excellent team of doctors, I had come to visit you every day from the mansion where we were being put up and, by way of the reflex movements of your body and the expression on your face artificially put to sleep, I intuited the nightmares, anxieties, anachronisms, abrupt change of subject and of characters, ambiguous location of the backgrounds, change of voices, vagueness and fragmentation of dream plots, the gradual insinuation of annihilation as an obsessive leitmotif, insidious crescendo that reached the point of climax, gesture of horror, vertigo of the abyss, scream stifled in the bottom of your throat immediately followed by a long pause, hypnogenetic levitation to an analgesic and happy scene, harmony, quiet, calm, serenity of your face, once the crisis was past, in the diffuse beatitude of trance

and all of that had been the effect of the medication, of the subtle combination of drugs which, according to what I was told, had been prescribed for me so as to alleviate the possible after-effects of the accident, the incomprehensible and spectacular fall from the stairway a few days (or hours?) following our arrival at that rest home with the appearance of a resort hotel?

yes, of course, the other said, the thud as you landed was tremendous, fortunately I had instantly lost consciousness and remained, would remain in a deep coma, sparing me the fright, anxiety and suffering of those who witnessed the event and were present at the time of my transfer to the operating room of the sanitorium close by, they awaited in suspense the results of the cranial x-ray and the consultation with the director of the traumatology team, an anguished, hours-long wait as you continued to lie peacefully in limbo, don't worry, they said, though he's been very close to passing on to a better life he was saved by a miracle and will be staying on here with us poor mortals, unless God, in his infinite goodness, decides other-wise, exactly that, in those very terms, laughing to dispel natural fears and lend a bit of courage, in view of the seriousness of the blow lethargy is a normal reaction and we will keep a close watch on how it develops until he recuperates, the process will be a slow one, so don't worry, within a few days I'll be able to return to the mansion and continue my marvelous summer vacation with you, as you've been able to see for yourself the clinic is close by, we have everything necessary at our disposal here

as in the days of our vaguely remembered arrival, now long
past, we went out for a stroll in mid-morning, I walked arm in
arm now as a precaution against another unfortunate stumble
or the vertigo that came over me at times, a probable after-
effect of the fall or prolonged medication, we went directly
downstairs from our room in the elevator avoiding the slippery
wooden stairs, crossed the deserted lobby and returned the
friendly smile of the staff or the chambermaids, it was a
splendid day and invited one to walk carefully between the
flower beds and borders, little by little I was regaining the
memory of the mansion in which we were staying, of the main
building bundled up in ivy against the cold and the more
modern and tasteless pavilion with the dining room and the
recreation, gymnasium and massage facilities

(there where, to my great surprise, one of the matrons dressed
as a nurse had invited me to get on an old drugstore scale,
carefully recorded my weight in a notebook and suggested that
she give me a thorough therapeutic massage, an offer I politely
but firmly refused

I'm in fine shape, I said, accompanying the phrase with
explanatory gestures so that she'd understand me

her hands were big and rough, with a threatening look of
brutality)

the other guests had gone off early in the morning in a bus, on
the way to a private beach, leaving the park and its shaded
walks to lovers of meditation or surly obscurity, enjoying the
usufruct of a precarious peace eternally threatened by the
unexpected return of the bathers, couples, families, noisy
progeny, a small multitude launching an assault on the lounge
chairs and canvas mattresses, anxious to prolong until the little
bell announcing lunch their inelegant exposure to the sun in
their dark glasses, remaindered beach hats and the inevitable
plastic sheath over the already peeled bridge of their noses,
look, you'd think they were Martians the other said on the first
day, their uncouth lack of physical grace had disconcerted us

and we didn't know whether to attribute these traits to their usual diet or to the obligatory sedentary nature of their profession, that immodest exhibition of ugliness and self-neglect perturbed us, what in the name of Lenin was the purpose of the household magazines they read, the other said, didn't they offer advice, as in the rest of the world, as to how to keep one's figure and lose weight?, it was impossible to answer these questions and we confined ourselves to exchanging looks of complicity and gestures of dismay with the few peripatetics, annoyed, as we were, at the daily commotion caused by their intrusion

subtle bonds of connivance beyond linguistic barriers, educational conventions and the ambiguous nature of our status (were we official guests, did we hold some high rank or post?), a barely perceptible smile or a slight raising of the eyebrows when the beach crowd rushed to the dining room tables next to the windows or the empty seats of the bus that took them back to the beaches following their afternoon nap, a vague sensation of spiritual affinity which, by distinguishing us from the others, naturally excluded us from the sphere of their occupations and interests, indirectly conferring on us a unique aura of dignity

> an older gentleman of distinguished bearing and a straw
> hat, who ceremoniously bared his head as he greeted us
> a young professor of Arabic
> the prior of a Greek monastery absorbed in the reading of
> the Canticle
> a seminarian with a pious air, the attendant or familiar of
> the Archimandrite
> a Kirghiz of indefinable age dressed in striped pajamas
> an angular lady in elegant attire and a lighted Philippine
> cigarette at the end of her long amber holder

on our first walk through the garden grove after my absurd fall, we had come upon the prior, the lady and the seminarian and, in a discreet way, the three of them manifested their happiness at seeing me again, at knowing that I had recovered from the trauma and the sleep cure, fancy that, they're positively beaming, the other said, while you were in a coma they were obviously worried, they gazed at me in silence with a questioning look, someone had told them the circumstances surrounding what happened and, in a circumspect way, they tried to comfort me, express their sympathy and their solidarity then later, in the dining room, we spied the Kirghiz and the professor of Arabic lost in the puerile hubbub of the other diners, we returned their greeting from a distance but the older gentleman in the straw hat was not in the corner he ordinarily occupied, he vanished on the very day of your accident, the other said, and nobody has seen hide nor hair of him since, his abrupt departure struck me as odd, and as they were serving us the usual tasteless menu (the rubbery sadness of the chicken inclined one to think that the poor creature had hastened its predictable end by means of a coldly pre-meditated suicide) I decided, I announced, to investigate his disappearance

how, through whom, by what means?

I'll summon the interpreter!

impossible, the other said, he was off on vacation for a few days and his substitute was an obtuse man of few words, whose official motto appeared to be secrecy, the stubborn refusal to give out any information

all this is absurd, couldn't something have happened to him?

forget it, the other said, in the situation we're in at present, we'd best let sleeping dogs lie and keep our mouths shut like the others in the capital they had emphasized the advantages over the hotel, you'll be among your fellows there, as they say, you can have discussions with them and profit from exchanging information and ideas with colleagues, the accommodations may not be as comfortable but the service is impeccable, you will have tranport available to go to the beaches and a team of doctors and nurses will be at your disposal night and day if you fear you have contracted an illness or feel the need to cure yourself of an addiction, a new, more healthful and rational, conception of summer vacations, in this rest home you will immediately strike up friendships and get to know our people, we're all like one big family

cheerful words which, as we leaned on the balustrade of the terrace decorated with large pots of hydrangeas, we contrasted with the reality of the panorama facing us, the horde of boarders slumped in the deck chairs and on the mattresses, paunches exposed to the sun, smeared with suntan oil, legs spread obscenely, in bathing suits and sun hats, dark glasses and plastic noses, if they're professors they don't look like it, the other remarked for the hundredth time, I'm sure they've never read a book in their life, and as though corroborating that opinion, the individual dressed in a sweat shirt and gym pants began his terrifying muscle-flexing exercises, during your cure he had sat beside me once in the bus and I noticed that he was armed, he had a revolver in his beach bag and when he opened it to devour a patently stale mortadella sandwich, he didn't even bother to hide it

are all of them colleagues of mine?, I had asked the interpreter before the accident, my curiosity appeared to have taken him by surprise, and somewhat puzzled, he explained that the residence also took in persons who had come from very different horizons, having expressed their desire to make our acquaintance and share our experience, although they have rest homes the same as or better than this one they had opted for a change of air and chosen to come here, as you can see we follow an accommodating method favoring mobility and interchange, my compatriots wish to take advantage of the summer to extend their relations to other spheres, to break the isolation and monotony of excessive specialization

although it was getting late and the already moderate sun grazed the tops of the trees in its descending trajectory, the beachniks, as we sarcastically baptized them, wished in their greed to reap the dubious benefit of its last rays, some of them remained standing, turned toward it, with their arms slightly open and the palms of their hands extended in a posture of mute surrender or adoration, the greasy shine of the sunscreen cream, dark glasses and plastic noses added to the scene an unreal and vaguely fantastic glint, reminiscent of a science fiction film, the other said, or of one of those publicity videos in which hundreds of people pouring out of subway exits wearing glasses with mirror lenses in bizarre frames walk along in silence, with resolute step, to the entrance of a big department store and there, with an energetic gesture, take off their masks and manifest with an ineffable smile their pleasure and happiness at what they've discovered, the Eureka of their paradise found at last, the comparison delighted me, the red sun, surrounded by little pink clouds, gave the obese actors with displeasing physiques a mocking resemblance to priests or vestals of the abolished cult, senatresses proud of their recent visit to the sanctified spot, in a solemn act of thanksgiving for the honey of the gift received, ardent communion in the tabernacle of the anointed one, purified after the lustral bath, fortified by the virtue and the offering of their lovers, swaggering and agile despite their advanced age and obesity, rejuvenated finally by their return to the domains of the mistress, the Lady in her votive altar at the counter, marvelous temple of love, Sauna of Saunas

the lady with the amber cigarette holder lighted with deliberate slowness one of her extremely long cigarettes, she too scrutinized the tribe without indulgence as it avariciously

squeezed the last ray out of its planet, exchanged with us a look
of disdain and pointed to the strip of sea barely visible through
the dense verdure of the pines
the Hellespont, she said, wasn't that where the emperor
banished Ovid?

her observation finally provided us with a clue
neither in the capital where we made plans for the trip nor on
our arrival at the summer residence had they given us any
precise indication as to the location of the rest home, its
climate was typically southern, quite similar to that of the
beaches that we always went to, with August temperatures
fluctuating between twenty and thirty degrees centigrade, nor
did the vegetation differ from the sort with which we were
familiar, plane trees, pines, cypresses mingled with the hardiest
and most far-reaching of the more Nordic species, from the
balustrade of the main building we focused the binoculars on
routine coastal views, white sailboats, little passenger steamers,
the incongruous silhouette of an ocean liner whose prow
emerged diaphanously from between the trees, I would like to
tour the other said, go on an excursion for a few hours, change
the ritual of these interminable vacations, there was an old map
in color hanging in the lobby next to the three-piece living
room suite where the beachniks gathered after dinner to absorb
the tv images and we devoted ourselves to contemplating the
map, look, Rumelia, its northern principalities are Walachia
and Moldavia, the discovery captivated us and we returned to
the terrace in a state of somnambulistic bliss, we had to find the
interpreter right away, ask him to telephone to the state tourist
agency, request an official permit and reserve a car, I'll take
care of everything the other said, and meanwhile, settled
comfortably in your deck chair among the pots of hydrangeas,
you return the polite greeting of the prior of the Greek
monastery when he crosses the terrace followed by the
seminarian, the exegesis of the reformer appears to be torturing
him and from a distance you will see him get involved in a
hermeneutic controversy with the young professor of Arabic
an unexpected problem has arisen, the interpreter says, they
have just stopped traffic on the expressway along the coast
because there in a public works project under way to widen it
and, for the moment, we can't go anywhere

isn't there another inland highway that goes up to the
mountains?
it's cut off too
then the steamship lines that
that service has been suspended
has there been some sort of accident or catastrophe?
we have the situation well under control, everything is perfectly
normal
we were thinking that perhaps
what do you mean by that?
who, me?
yes, you, your plural baffles me, as far as I know there is no one
with you
is he me? am I her? and so on for hours, wide awake, tossing
and turning in confusion, anxiously clutching the pillow,
plunged into the fiery brightness of the dark night, the
antechamber of an opaque dawn, the gentle threshold of
ecstatic intoxication

was it possible to decipher the obscurities of the text, find a univocal explanatory key, get to the bottom of its occult sense through recourse to allegory, circumscribe its linguistic ambiguities, establish a rigorous philological critique, search out a strictly literal meaning, resort to moral and anagogical interpretations, straighten out its malleable syntax, elucidate its supposed absurdities, extenuate its abrupt and unparalleled radicality, structure, order, prune, reduce, strive to trap its immensity and fluidity, capture the subtlety of wind in a net, immobilize its ungraspable fluctuations and oneiric shifts, reproduce the pure splendor of the mystic fire through the accumulation of glosses, commentaries, index cards, academic notes and comments, leaden observations, stodgy syntactical arrangements, filtered exegeses, pages and pages of dull and redundant prose?

wouldn't it be better to plunge once and for all into the infinitude of the poem, accept the impenetrability of its mysteries and opacities, free your own language from the shackles of rationality, abandon it to the magnetic field of its secret attractions, encourage the wave of its expansion, admit plurality and simultaneity of meaning, purify the verbal incandescence, the flame and gentle cautery of its living love?

passage after passage of enigmatic beauty, incoherency revealing of the intoxication and joyful consummation of the soul, esoteric connection to the Kabbala and Sufi experience, daring appropriation of the Other in the verse Beloved transformed into Lover!

it suffices to change posture, lean your head to the right or left, modify the numbing position of your legs owing to the excessive softness of the bed or the slackness of the springs of the mattress on which you have been lying since your nebulous accident

(as uncomfortable in its affable and indolent old age as a rheumatoid water bed)

in order to perceive the unmistakable odor of their lubricated bodies, vinelike arms, muscles of smooth and glossy hardness, to sense the watchful presence of their prey close by, crude union of the embrace, sinuous subjection of lovers and surrender to the inner vision of their strong backs, glistening bent shoulder blades, sumptuous texture of intertwined members, slow mutual devouring, two burly bruisers anointed to the edge of their stout leather shorts, oil and sweat intermingled, smoke longing for one who does not give off fire, inflammatory concretion of your dream, ardent desire for shared possession, soothing massage of your battered thorax with oil poured out by the jar bearers, diffuse calm transmuted into happiness, alchemy, dilation, heat, voluptuous pleasure, light, annihilation the late afternoons wore on, the sun had apparently interrupted its illusory orbital motion and, for some time now, seemed to be decorating the upper edge of the pines and firs alongside the balustrade, a reddish disk of suspect weightlessness dyed the landscape in a gaudy orange tone, the bits and pieces of sea, the shady grove, the garden, and in the foreground, the lawn on which the beachniks were savoring the exquisiteness of the extension of time with importunate hands outstretched, eager to store up its deceptive gift, the dark glasses with bright-colored frames and the plastic noses giving them the appearance of Cyranos accentuated the hieraticism and ritualism of the scene, were they colleagues actors zombies aborigines of a remote and unexplored island?, the patently artificial light of the fixed planet gradually suffused them with an excessive and garish redness, it shone on the lenses and nose shields of their protective face masks, were they devoting themselves, as you had believed in the beginning, to a puerile and exaggerated cult of Phoebus or were they protecting themselves, as the lady with the amber cigarette holder had whispered in your ear, from the irradiation to which the two of you were being carelessly exposed, the isotopes and volatile bodies that covered the entire area and, apparently, were contaminating it?

they aren't saying anything so as not to scare off the foreign tourist trade but they're in on the secret and are taking protective measures that we know nothing about

her information, passed on in confidence, although uncertain, had increased your fear, what in fact were those beachniks doing there, rooted for hours in front of that violet-colored light that didn't even come from the pasteboard sun but from light bulbs cleverly hidden by the stage designer amid the arborescences of the make-believe grove of trees?, had they been warned of the danger and, out of cowardice, keeping the two of you in ignorance?

you focused your binoculars on them and inspected one by one, with growing apprehension, their gross faces, impenetrable and stubborn, their glasses with mirror lenses of a changeable and outlandish design, their plastic noses of obscene and inordinate thickness

(what was Don Blas doing among them, in diguise too in that ridiculous attire of his?)

the ladies gathered on the terrace showed off their finery and plumed hats, complained of the tedium and heat, snapped their fans open swiftly and abruptly, suggested storytelling and parlor games to counter the numbing daily routine

they looked at you

made up like a mask, stylized eyelashes and eyelids, mascara, rouge, rice powders, aggressively scarlet heart-shaped lips

the flashiest one in the group had sidled up next to you and took you familiarly by the arm

I'm the ambassadress of your country, she said, come with me and we'll take a stroll, I want to show you by yourself, slowly and carefully, the deep secrets of the park

you cross arm in arm the threshold of the legation, the little
gate guarded by chauffeurs and servants, the gravel walk next
to the ambassador's Ottoman villa, the esplanade with antique
cars so as to mix with the imposingly dressed collection of
guests gathered together on the lawn, he's a compatriot of ours
she says, though he vibrates, suffers and yearns in far-distant
lands, he shares our principles and ideas, he believes in the
perpetuity of our essences and the virtues of the Movement for
regeneration, the other guests bend down to shake your hand
and you exchange politenesses with them, many are wearing
tuxedos or morning coats but there is also an abundance of
military jackets, boots, cassocks, blue and scarlet shirts and
berets, chests augustly bemedaled, the majestic finery of a
gondolier or a tenor, come on, hurry it up, get in formation, the
chaplain orders with a clap of his hands, war veterans preceding
groups of young people, daisies, stars, arrows, true-blue
Scouts, all in a row, their right hand on the shoulder of the
male or female comrade directly in front of them, maintaining
their distances, erect, very erect, saluting the holy image of the
Virgin, the forever blessed Mother of God
the procession majestically descends the flight of cement steps
around the delicate little statue, Don Blas with his gait of a
militant prelate, surrounded by acolytes and girls and boys in
uniform, Doña Urraca and her fellow propagandists, actors
and extras with faces withdrawn from the world since
childhood, remember that we are in mission country and must
evangelize through example, show the infidels the luminous
way of beliefs for which thousands upon thousands of innocent
and ardent youths generously offered their lives amid the din of
battle
(you don't know how you are dressed and will never know
do you have on the same informal clothes you wore in the rest
home or have you had time to change?)
the ambassador, the ambassador's wife, civil and military
attachés, hierarchs of the party, representatives of the powers

that be on these remote shores head the procession directly behind the flamboyant chaplain dressed with all the pomp that the occasion demands, cope, ring, crosier, solemn and hieratic, accompanied by deacons and altar boys in snow-white tunics, prayers, offerings and vows to the Virgin, an anemic, ailing nymphet borne on a portable platform through the vast garden of the legation shaded by its leafy grove of trees, on the way to the artificial grotto where the little statue will be enthroned during the ceremony, glorification of the Virgin Patroness on this symbolic date commemorated by believers throughout the world now that our fatherland has recovered its vigor and grandeur, vanquished those who were its enemies for centuries both within and without, swept its ancestral soil clean, extirpated the seeds of disunion and impiety sown by deadly doctrines, the hoarse and battle-hardened voice of Don Blas in his beret and leggings of bygone days, seated in the rocking chair in the salon, the object of mute and respectful fervor, in all likelihood following the recital of the rosary and special ejaculatory prayers for the family dead

(who was it that allowed the boy to peek from the balcony? haven't I told all of you a thousand times that I don't want him to see?)

prayers echoed in chorus by the throats of children and adults on the sloping lawn of the garden, dignitaries, deacons, altar boys, uniformed young people wearing emblems, Doña Urraca girdled in her aureole of the inflexible war widow (wasn't the youngster whom she had aided with a handful of coins and a bowl of porridge an orphan and the son of one of those on the other side?), ladies escaped from the nearby seaside resort, the Archimandrite and his familiar, the young and elegant professor of Arabic, all gravely hymning the praise of the nymphet, come on, louder, your voices must convey the grandeur and serenity of the message to the invertebrate mass of infidels and atheists, to those who insist upon denying the sacred evidence of our Cause, as the procession winds through the grove, approaches the moss-covered grotto and the bare staffs on which the flags are about to be raised, who said that she was no longer Catholic? ominous memory of a sinful statement that Don Blas forcefully refutes, all gathered together now round the nymphet in the clearing in the wood, a phalanx of youths with their bugles and drums, the officiating priest, ambassadors, dignitaries, provosts, authorities, hier- archies, as in the raging tide of the plaza some forty years back, under his uncles' balcony, upraised arms, speeches, hymns, public sessions of purification and exorcism, ashen air and the acrid odor of something burning, corrupt manuscripts thrown into the fire, harmful ideas, perverse utopias, fake-sounding promises meant to trap unwary souls and cast them forever into the abyss, page upon page of small print condemned by the redeeming zeal of the chaplain and Doña Urraca, blackened and twisted in a few seconds by the providential action of the flames

(who had their author been?

could the poet have witnessed from his cell some similar book-burning or expurgation?)

prayers, murmurs, ceremony of the dedication of the country to its holy Patroness, virile unfurling of flags in the wind, orations and discourses of captivating eloquence until the conclusion of the service and the guiding of the select gathering to the buffet served by uniformed domestics, hackneyed comments on the beauty and emotion of the prelate's homily intermingled with venomous criticisms of the Greek prior's seminarian for his girlish falsettos and his shocking pink garters had they remained motionless the whole time, turned toward the sun simulated by the stage designer on the pasteboard backdrop suspended behind the arborescences of the painted grove of trees?

their robot-like hieraticism, bodies smeared with sun-filtering creams, dark glasses in bizarre shapes, prominent plastic noses conferred on the grotesque tribe of beachniks an unreal and threatening aura, emphasized by the disinfectant lotion with which certain of them, after brushing their sports outfits, energetically scrubbed the ground

those of us excluded from these means of secret prophylaxis stood leaning on the balustrade of the terrace, fascinated as well by the immobility of the scene, the false fixed planet, the sea views outlined amid the pines, the growing sensation of emptiness and confinement

were there plans for general evacuation, as the lady with the amber cigarette holder maintained or were they simply keeping us separated from the others on account of our readings or our blood tests?

the indefinite prolongation of the day, change in the schedule for meals, sudden inexplicable absence of the employees of the rest home who ordinarily served us contributed to the increasing uneasiness and alarm among those gathered on the terrace, the Kirghiz in the striped pajamas anxiously consulted a dictionary as though he wanted to ask questions or speak at last to us, the professor of Arabic had given up his study of the volume of Ibn Al Farid and was closely watching with obvious apprehension the exercises of the beachniks, automatic movements of arms and legs, torsos tilting, inhalations-exhalations of mechanical deep breathing orchestrated by the instructor dressed in a sweat shirt and gym shorts, pure war of nerves waged by the prior of the Greek monastery or preamble to another aggression still more treacherous and vague?

I would like to speak with you for a few minutes, you say to him pardon my frankness, but is your proposal a personal initiative of yours or did you request permission to converse with me for a while?

in view of the similarity of our preoccupations and experiences I thought

I'm sorry, but in that case I cannot communicate with you

the Archimandrite abruptly turns his back on you and the seminarian languidly blinks his eyelashes, isn't it enough for you to know what happened to the gentleman in the straw hat? in hard times like these learn to leave us in peace!

and all by yourself once more at the balustrade of the terrace, caught in the voluble hubbub of the ladies, absorbed in watching the beachniks and their absurd preparations for war, confused as well by the red disk of the sun, the deceptive quiet of the garden, the grove of trees of captivating artificiality, a conspiracy of foreboding signs of the imprecise threat that is lurking, plague, radiation, virus, premonition of death, sudden predicted intrusion of the unkempt one-syllable apparition with her long skinny legs and fantastic scarecrow silhouette why had they put the reproduction of the painting precisely there?

done in soft lacquer by an artist with visionary powers, its seemingly discreet malignity insidiously contaminated the room, steeped its atmosphere in a subtle and poisonous anxiety

what significance to attribute to that allegory of the Fate sowing discord hanging on the wall of your room, a scant three meters from the head of the bed in which, after your inexplicable fall, you remained in a feverish and confused state, vainly endeavoring to quiet your nerves?

try not to look at it, the other said, the nurse will be along in a few minutes and she'll give you an injection, and you'll see, you'll sleep like an angel

but how to take your eyes off her, in her black broad-brimmed hat, veiled face, cape with the loose folds of a shroud, filiform extremities, heavy, bulky clogs, of enormous gravitational force?

she looked at you, she looked at both of you through her long disheveled locks, with her eyes hidden in the underbrush flashing and incandescent, pupils searching and voracious, expert at the art of glimpsing through the tangle of veils the components of the scene and its bewildered actors, glacial presence and subduing proximity of the beanpole of a woman framed in the room, with no indication as to the author and date

had you asked the doctor and nurses to take it away?, it seemed to you that that was how you remembered it, but it was the other way around, you insisted that they leave it, said the voice, you assured them that her image diverted and calmed you, after the trauma you needed to fix your attention on something and her widow's veils, limp limbs, lap pregnant with celluloid dolls and discordant ugliness of a scarecrow offered you diversion and solace, those were difficult days in which you were barely able to move, your sickness threatened to spread, the tranquilizers kept you outwardly drowsy, in a phase of secret and fertile receptivity amid fits of delirium, oneiric chaos and a somnambulistic lack of a sense of time, you kept repeating phrases that seemed disconnected at first, you lovingly chided the poet, reproached him for the insoluble enigma of the Canticle, adopted his tense, fragmented turns of phrase, traversed the hallucinatory geography of his verses, his insular and ecstatic spaces, overcome with fears and messianic raptures, fluctuating between the freedom and the gloom of his spiritual night

disturbing images, sudden flickers of memory, gradual dis-
sipation of the fog, victim of an accident, sick, radiated,
subjected to the normalizing therapy of an inquisitorial prison
with the pampered luxury and qualities of a clinic?, rapid and
evanescent remembrance of the older gentleman in his straw
hat entering your bedroom with his index finger on his lips as a
sign of secrecy, a message barely whispered with his face
distorted by terror, have you realized, has it occurred to you
where we are?, just as the maid responsible for the cleanliness
and order of that floor bursts into the room at his heels and
grabs him rudely by the arm, come, professor, can't you see that
you're bothering this distinguished foreign guest?, a foggy and
unreal apparition in the half-sleep of a nocturnal anxiety
pregnant with questions, minutes or hours before your fall on
the stairs, in bed still but with your ear alert to the sounds
filtering in from outside, on the beachniks absorbed in the
execution of their peculiar self-defense exercises, what were
they doing standing in front of the artificial planet at midnight
with their farcical look of penguins and their warrior spirit?,
had they been invited by error to the congress of commentators
and exegetes of the mysticopoetic experience or were the
persons there by error you and the half-dozen terrified and
evasive specialists whom you ran into every day there,
overwhelmed by the weight of the more and more oppressive
and tense atmosphere?, the texts of speeches handed over to the
organizers of the meeting, your intuitive reconstruction of the
Treatise on the Qualities of the Solitary Bird given to the
interpreter weeks before to be translated, photocopied and
distributed among the other colleagues had not been returned
to you, the activities announced in the program were
inexplicably put off till some later time, your questions or
complaints received no response and no one even apologized for
the fact that your notes and drafts had been confiscated, was it
the urgent desire to know and have things settled, to find out
why you were there and what was really happening behind your

back that impelled you to get up out of bed, dress yourself, put on your shoes, spy from the window on the maneuvers of the militia of beachniks smeared with sun lotion, to throw the curves and graphs of your dubious viral infection onto the floor, to investigate the possible radiation of the area and the consequent adoption of precautionary measures?, be careful, the one with the long amber cigarette holder said, our hearts are with you, an electric light hidden by the stage designer in the flies and suspended scenery illuminated the inside of the room but did not reach as far as the corridor and you went down it in the dark feeling your way perceiving behind you the muffled footsteps of doctors and nurses, arduous ascent from abysmal depths in search of light and air, room to breathe, nearing the cool mornings you had chosen, the more certain light of midday, drowned in a bath of subtle delight

and then voices, guttural orders, the unstable image of the beachnik in sweat shirt and gym shorts crouching at the top of the staircase, brandishing in the shadows a length of wood or a stake, brutal blow, loss of balance, sensation of rolling and rolling in the spiral of the whirlpool, drawn to the vortex of Aminadab by the torrential force of the waters

as in a dream within a dream within a dream but wholly awake
I perceived, you perceived the hoarse, raucous din, the muffled
tide of voices

persistent echo though subject to variations of volume and
tone, as if someone, from some remote control center, were
checking the microphones before a performance or proceeding
to conduct a hearing test on a patient affected by deafness

a mere murmur or buzz whose intensity, instead of tracing a
straight or gently broken line, was making crude zigzags like an
electrocardiogram gone mad, brief silences or pauses full of
tension before the collectivity emitting the sound broke in
unison into a roar, an ay! brusquely interrupted by an unknown
event or one prolonged to the extreme, into a sort of sullen,
visceral bellow, like that of an animal being sacrificed in the
slaughterhouse

minutes or hours lying in wait for that lying in wait, the sudden
sea-swell of voices that seemed to emanate from the stands of a
nearby stadium since the sound came straight through the thick
stone walls and, flowing down the long windowless corridor,
reached his cell through the arrow loophole, a game between
rivals in the first division as he had once heard the jailer remark
to the Inspector or a friar?, the local team against one from a
rival town? or perhaps a sports competition of greater scope
and import?, the impassioned state of that crowd jammed
together, fused into a single organism, with simultaneous and
concordant reactions, led one to believe, led you to believe in
the transcendence of what was at stake, laurels or a recompense
the attainment of which would offer the victor an almost
ecumenical prestige, how otherwise to explain the unusual
conjoining of wills, shared inner vibration, coordinated vocal
movements, leaping hearts and racing pulses, inflammation,
hypnotic trance, possession?

the sound track of the crowd milling about in the stands,
communicants with one and the same fervor fearing neither
sleet nor hail, defined by its ruptures, developments, rises and

falls an otherwise incommensurable time, relieved the anxiety
that overwhelmed me, broke the solitude and oppression of an
area whose exact limits and location I knew nothing of but
could imagine on the basis of the nocturnal sorties when,
escorted by the guard, I was taken to the refectory to fast and be
subjected to the circular discipline of the friars
it mattered little that the howling went on in a disquieting
fashion well beyond the natural effusion that follows upon
some victory or glorious feat on the part of the native
inhabitants, its warm and palliative effect, produced by
thousands of throats, calmed my anxiety in the face of the
ordeal and the endless delays of the trial that awaited me

into the deep caverns of the senses, dark and blind, there suddenly burst in with lighted lamps a group of Unreformed Carmelite friars, dozens of laymen, men at arms, their cutting voices raised, their threatening tone growing louder as they drew nearer, refused entry they had forced the main door bolt by bolt, giving him time to tear up his papers and swallow the most dangerous ones, I'm coming. I'm coming, in a minute, in a minute, as the friars beat on his cell door and managed to break it open, flung themselves on him and his companion, dragged them to a monastery in irons, exhibited their prey in the choir and had them flogged by the guards

was it true, had he read that scene in a book or was it a persistent nightmare?

my back ached, as though in the black chamber of the abominable ones I had abandoned myself once more to the fluctuations of my secret gravitation, to intermingled suffering and beatitude, to consummate bliss, but the narrow space in which I woke up, after a dream-trip through rugged lands via rough paths, did not correspond to that of the cells in which, filled with delicious knowledge and lulled to sleep by the whispering of those dressed in togas, I regained consciousness of my delights in the garden of the Lady, a hole some six feet wide and ten feet long built into a wall of solid granite, with a single niggardly embrasure opening onto the semidarkness of the corridor

nor did the wretched bed of bare planks, torn and dirty blankets or the big bowl of ashes that at first I took to be a bowl of water bear any relationship to the disposition of the prayer stools in the little cells on which we composed ourselves and knelt to receive the liqueur, the sweet sacramental seed, with that meticulous repetition of pious souls who, once the exercises and prayers to the saint of their particular devotion have been completed, eagerly proceed to other chapels, with an ardor and longing difficult to satisfy

(might they have brought him there at night with his eyes

blindfolded after making their way through steep and narrow streets, forcing him to turn round and round in circles so as to disorient him and keep him from recognizing the way in accordance with the decisions of the monastic chapter and the orders of the Apostolic Nuncio?)

plunged in shadow as the light from the embrasure paled and the oil lamp did not yet light the vault of the underground corridor, he listened, pricking up his ears, in a state of receptive suspense and serenity, to the dull roar of the crowd, the howls and the hue and cry from the stadium clad in a rough sheepskin coat reaching down to his knees, without habit or hood or scapular, was the grotesque disguise not the one most suited to his desires to express his profound disapproval of the farce of a world irredeemably condemned to disaster?, he had already gone through a thousand deaths so as to leave the prison of the body and of a corruptible universe that would dry up like hay, his shackles were worth more than a thousand crowns and prepared as he was to suffer any and every torment, the tempting offers of a priorate, a spacious cell, access to a library with ancient manuscripts, not only in Greek and Latin but also in Hebrew and Arabic, had not weakened his will or affected his firm resolve, better rags, stink, swill, the contempt of the community, a diet of bread and water, circular discipline, reprimands, insults, interrogations through the door of his dungeon

(he listened to the Vicar General and his party as they scrutinized endless genealogies without realizing the real meaning of the doctrine, that all was dust and would return to dust and, at the hour of passing on, alone with their works and deeds, they would be neither punished nor redeemed by the blood of their ancestors)

dead Christians rather than Old Christians, obeying rules laid down by choir and bell, they swallowed the camel and strained out the gnat, mistook chaff for grain, sought the presence of the Beloved in a temple of stone and did not find it in their heart of hearts, in the substance of their living temples!

the voice of the jailer, conversing with the friars, broke the silence of his narrow hole, the routine of hours measured by the greater or lesser intensity of the light that filtered through the embrasure, the initial threats of causing him to disappear by throwing him down a well had given way to more ordinary subjects of conversation, the daily headings of the breviary or missal, the refectory diet of dried vegetables, cleanliness of the chamber pots interspersed sometimes with speculations as to the mysterious plague that was infecting certain quarters of the city or commentaries on the immediate disclosure by the turnbox monk of the result of the game in the stadium

he observed that the refectorian, on pushing through the opening of the cell door his usual ration of turnips and lentils, wore nurse's gloves and had his face covered with a gauze mask

surprised at that unexpected innovation in the jail regime, he stood there lost in thought, not picking up the little bowl from the floor and his eyes, on meeting mine, had in them for the first time an expression of forlornness and puzzlement

what was the meaning of those precautions, the cordon sanitaire placed about his cell by the Unreformed Carmelites? was his contagion also physical or, as he had believed up until then, merely spiritual?

how and when had he slipped inside the cell?

on opening his eyes or changing position on the miserable straw mattress on which he was lying, he had suddenly spied him dressed with all the pomp of great solemn occasions, cope edged with feathers, plumed miter of a cuirassier, pastoral ring and crosier in the form of a scepter, imploring him with gestures and miming to speak softly, to not disturb the silence, he had come from far, very far away, from the garden rest home, to warn him and comfort him, using all sorts of stratagems to get into the monastery and lull the friars' suspicions, a risky journey, full of traps and dangers, till he found him and the dungeon in which they had buried him, he had looked over the minutes of the chapter of the Order and its accusations, though groundless, were very grave, he was accused of being mendacious, contumacious, deceptive and blasphemous, of having upheld with great pertinacity and Luciferian pride, reviling the learned doctors and authorities, a multitude of erroneous, offensive, contumelious and heretical propositions, of following the diabolical path of the Ophites, Carpocratians, Nicolaitans, Adamites, Priscillianists and other precursors of the contemporary illuminati, estranged, enraptured and transported, of seeking to maintain the soul in a suspended state of complete quiet, of discarding the simulacra of vocal prayer and every external show of devotion, of annihilating the will and yielding to the filthiness of carnal appetites the better to mortify the affections, they had sent emissaries to the principal higher schools of learning of the Orient to request information about the Shadilis, they are convinced that there exist secret points of convergence between your poems and those of the visionaries and mystics of the poisonous Mohammedan sect, their spies are in the process of carefully examining the theses on the subject and are openly photocopying and seizing our papers, the older gentleman in the straw hat whom we chanced upon from time to time in the spa was kidnapped and subjected to the torture of the cord and

the water jar, they were trying to get his glosses of the texts of
Ibn Arabi and Ibn Al Farid out of him but, put on his guard by
my familiar, he swallowed the most compromising ones and
flushed the others down the toilet, the young professor of
Arabic was able to make himself scarce in time and is now
hiding from the prior of the Order and the violence of his hired
assassins, he wanted to communicate with you at all costs and
see that you received a coded message which, at the last
moment, in the necessary haste of his flight, he did not manage
to hand over to me, these are very hard times, the roads and
borders are very closely watched, secret informers raid towns in
search of prey, those suspected of being stricken with disease
are subjected to blood tests and rounded up in sports stadiums,
when they come to interrogate you don't say one word about
my visit, the proofs they have available for bringing the case to
trial are still flimsy and your defense must dispute any
connection with previous heresies that have been condemned,
the multiform language and infinite possible meanings of your
verses have them completely bewildered, the confusion of
spaces, times, subjects and characters has caught them up in a
waking dream from which they are vainly attempting to free
themselves, avoid above all else telling them about the dark
night with the black chamber of our ecstasies and passionate
loves, the Lady's Turkish bath is still scaled shut and the ones
who survived the visit of the grotesque specter, the one with
endlessly long thin legs, may be summoned at any moment to
establish the facts, our fortunate presence on those premises,
the slightest imprudence on your part, a literal interpretation
of the "let us proceed farther into the underbrush" risks
putting them on our track and feeding the flames of the fire
that they're readying for us, my familiar has seduced the jailer
with his pretty seminarian's tunic and pink garters, but the
patrol of friars will be along soon and oblige me to interrupt
my apostolic mission, don't say a word, don't answer, don't
look at me, turn around and close your eyes, the indispensable

has been said, let us not prolong our meeting or linger over this matter, I shall wait till you're asleep before I steal out of this horrible jail for some time now, the roar of thousands of throats has kept rising in tone but the din with which the spectators hailed the presumed winning goal or some decision of the referee in favor of the local team is being prolonged beyond what is reasonable and plausible, becoming after a few hours frankly unreal and beyond belief

can it be, as you have heard it said in the corridor outside your cell, that what is being held is a round to eliminate teams come from all over the world? or, as you are inclined to think now, simply the replay of a tape made during one of the matches, repeated again and again, out of laziness and negligence on the part of the jailer?

the roar of a beast whose throat is being cut that breaks the silence and the fervent reaction it arouses nonetheless point to more violent and cruel hypotheses, celebrations of ritual murder, torture and sacrifice of animals, offerings to placate the Divinity, savage mutilations and fiendish agonies

had the Archimandrite been trying to alert you when, with her long cigarette quivering at the end of her amber holder, she murmured as though to herself, before disappearing, bread and circuses, thereby establishing a parallel between the amorality of the present era and that existing in the Rome of the Caesars?

but if the illusory sports competition were really a coverup for executions and killings, who were those condemned men in the pillory, sacrificed to the vindictiveness of a public ever eager to pour out a fluxus seminis at the sight of a fluxus sanguinis, handed over to the secular arm, subjected to being burned to death with viciously green wood, asphyxiated first by the smoke and then charred to a crisp by the flames? illuminati, poets, unbelievers, mystics, sorcerers, Judaizers, those guilty of the abominable sin?, did they lead them barefoot, dressed in the robe of a confessed heretic and wearing a cone-shaped hat, a gag, a rope around their neck and carrying a pale green candle in one hand, to the chapter of saintly men who had handed down the verdict and would piously exhort them one last time to repent before lighting the fire?, or were they sick women, victims of radiation, bearers of germs?

(they had destroyed their anthills and were aimlessly wandering about, pathetic and disoriented)

exhibited in cages, grotesquely disguised as pheasants or birds of paradise, as they emerged from the black chambers and nocturnal dens where they had been arrested?

what fate awaited you in that dark dungeon, famished and held incommunicado, object of abuse and threats so that you would reveal to their dull and narrow minds the ineffable nature of your experiences, the unequivocal meaning of your necessarily ambiguous verses pregnant with mystery, omni-valent metaphors, resistant to all restrictive and dogmatic interpretation?

an anxiety gnawed at and tormented you

had they recovered and reassembled in your little house of the Incarnation the fragments of the *Treatise on the Qualities of the Solitary Bird* that you had not had time to swallow and had only been able to tear up, leaving nothing but scattered scraps?

terrace with the balustrade of the rest home, faded deck chairs among large pots of hydrangeas, strip of sea barely visible amid the dense verdure of the pines, gesture of his hand indicating that there is no danger, no employee or nurse is patrolling anywhere about, the beachniks have disappeared, the day is mild and pleasant, only the lack of a breeze pervades the usually whispering firs with a strange and suspect quiet
the young professor of Arabic is simply dressed as is the custom in his native land, in his thin, ascetic face, enhanced by the thickness of his black beard and mustache, his eyes are bright translucent pools of light
my name is Ben Aïds, he says, you no doubt know of me or my name is familiar to you on account of the documents and books that you have consulted, it is a shame that a series of circumstances with which you are as well acquainted as I am has prevented us from communicating until today despite the fact of our living together for some time in this infernal resort, the authorities had accepted the idea of a symposium as a lesser evil, a means of maintaining a close watch on our movements and keeping us under control, the pluridisciplinary approach to the poetry of the saint is overwhelming them with anxiety, his ambiguous spiritual tessitura, the possible connection of his verses not only with traditional Jewish epithalamiums but also with the ecstasies and hallucinations of our mystics and illuminati made them fear that we had dragged them into a craggy terrain bristling with dangers, that of an area common to different and apparently contrary experiences, the mere idea of their secret affinities with the Mohammedan sect and the murk of blind paganism profoundly perturbed their souls, the prior and the inquisitors deemed the initiative to be blasphemous, how could a saint and a doctor of the Church have fallen into such absurd errors and extravagances?, not even friars who had fled from their monasteries and taken up with witches and whores had gone to such extremes of temerity!, it never entered their heads that, quite a few centuries back, our

poets too had preached the unitive way, the indispensable
reference to Ibn Arabi, Ibn Al Farid, Mawlana and Al Hallaj
confused and alarmed them, the radicality of a language that
was related to mystic intoxication, saliva commingled with
wine in the mouth of the Beloved, shook the very ground under
their feet, what to us is the needle pointing north that guides
and protects seamen is to them the embodiment of the innate
evil associated in their minds with the hated religion, the great
number of coincidences, similarity of images, conceptual
vagueness, breakdown of the system of equivalences, infinite
expansion of the meaning of the words grasped by the
commentators and exegetes of both camps seemed to them to
be the fruit of a perverse conspiracy against the embalmed
figure they zealously watch over, how to ready them for the
blinding brightness of a poetic vision capable of translating an
experience limitless in its effusions and outpourings, to make
them understand that the variety and fluidity of the states of
the soul in amorous trance can be expressed only by means of a
language as rich and complex as the one we find in the *Praise of
Wine*, the *Odes to Sham-Tabrizi* or the *Interpreter of Desires*,
to persuade them that the concepts and symbols of freedom and
confinement, ascent to the mountaintop, inner fountain,
lamps of fire or solitary bird on which a number of us are
working are in all probability not an indication of furtive
reading by the saint but of experiences converging on a rapture
and suspension of the senses foreign to the body of doctrines?,
their hired assassins had taken possession of our speeches and
were feverishly examining them, Don Blas invoked the spirit of
the Crusade and demanded an auto-da-fé of those impious
works, after detaining us on a thousand pretexts in the rest
home they openly showed their power and tried to intimidate
us, any error or imprudence gave them the chance they were
looking for, the older gentleman, the Archimandrite and his
familiar fell one after the other into the nets of their justice,
they had caught the seminarian in the black chamber of a sauna

and, on being subjected to torture, a witness stated that he had heard him exclaim in his joyous access of passion "why won't the Turk come and conquer this land so that everyone can live as they like?", a phrase which he admitted having uttered in the face of the threat of repeated immersion in a large earthen jar, was responsible for his severe sentence and it availed him nothing to have handed over to them in his terror the complete list of his accomplices and leveled delirious false charges against them, placed on public exhibition in the cage, along with the others who were contaminated, he was taken in a procession to the sports palace and delivered to the flames, their cries and laments of oh poor little me went on for minutes and minutes, didn't you hear them?, there was no way to escape them even though I had stopped up my ears and buried my head underneath a pile of pillows

on the empty stage set of the rest home not a leaf is moving and there is not a soul in sight

the silence! why this silence?

(were you the one who spoke, transforming the question into a sort of scream?)

didn't they tell you?, Ben Aïds says, the entire region has been evacuated, there is talk of a radioactive cloud to eliminate the virus but I don't trust a word they say, I was afraid that, if I didn't hide, they'd force me to climb into the trucks and take me to the stadium with the others if it were only a process of transference and psychopathic identification with the author of the work of so many loves and sorrows, as he smilingly maintained standing there alongside the head of my bed, why were they keeping me shut up in that damp, cruel cell?, did the hole six feet wide and ten long, the pallet of torn blankets, the thread of light tht filtered in from the corridor through the embrasure correspond, as he claimed with imperturbable serenity, to a description copied point for point from some treatise or reference book on the subject?, were the intrigues of the Carmelites in the refectory, veiled threats, invectives they rained down on the little charlatan-friar who was putting them in a ridiculous light, the blows administered by the community drawn up in a circle during the recitation of the Miserere, the persistent pain in my back as a result of the lashings given me by order of the Apostolic Nuncio also fantasies of mine, the fruit of a wild and sick imagination?, Ben Aïds had put me on my guard against the tricks and wiles they thought up, the use of medication, psychiatric sessions, recourse to drugs intended to alter the prisoner's normal perception and gradually sap his resistance, might the stubborn headache and the shooting pains on my left side not be after-effects of that refined and perverted treatment?, in such rough times, when the wolves of the Order were plotting against me, misinterpreting my verses and accusing me of saying things I never thought or said, how to have any faith in their diagnoses and medical treatments?, didn't the charges brought with such clever logic, cunning and malice that, even if true at times as far as my words and deeds went, were in the end entirely false, perhaps reveal the designs of the prior to put an end to the attempts at reform and our magnificent spiritual adventure?, were the interrogations to which they subjected me, rudely bursting into the cell with bailiffs and armed guards, a common ordinary dream as he asserted after taking my pulse or noting down my fever on his charts?, didn't his benign face take the place, in the well-known alternate hot-

and-cold tactic used by the police, of those who minutes before, without his conceit or presumption, had presented me with a long list of questions concerning doctrine, coercing me with their sudden presence and demanding that I explain them? didn't the verbal hallucination of my mystic poems contain erotic images of a manifest profane nature?, did I know the *Interpreter of Desires* and its way of transmitting the love-trance of the poet in a subtle and enigmatic language?, had I read the poetry of Ibn Al Farid and the commentaries of his exegetes?, was it true that barefoot novices of the reformed order recited the verses of "The Dark Night" and often sang them in chorus, accompanying themselves with rhythmic clapping of their hands, during recreation after meals?, had I also initiated them into the rapture of mystic states, the ritual whirling of suspensive and ecstatic dances?, did I know that Mawlana and his dervishes likewise aspired to wrench souls from their lethargy through dance, kindled in their ritual gatherings the soft and gentle flame of their fire, preached the intimate fusion of knowledge and love?, the most recent comparative studies that had come into their hands did not allow them to harbor the slightest doubt on the subject, they established with complete clarity the complicity existing between my doctrine and that of the sectarians of Islam

accusations, denunciations, vituperations of friars and inqui-sitors, paying no attention to reasons or replies, coming back again and again with deaf stubbornness to the question that I never stopped answering!

Don Blas, the unforgettable figure of Don Blas with his beret and leggings, fur-lined leather overcoat, blue shirt with crosses and medals, stamped into the house with heavy tread, surrounded, followed, cosseted by a cohort of women, maidservants aunts girl cousins, all eager to kiss his hand, to receive his precious benediction, to offer him some small service, encircled as he was in a flaming halo, warrior saint monk soldier, he gallantly denied his signs of fatigue, the day had been a hard one, all of it spent at the front raising the morale of our boys, comforting the wounded, charitably assisting prisoners who sought confession before being shot to death, a just and upright man, unbending when it came to principles but at the same time compassionate and tender-hearted, Doña Urraca used to say, carried away with emotion, I've seen him weep when an unfortunate lad refused his spiritual aid, he shut himself up in the officers' chapel and prayed and prayed the Lord to take pity on him and welcome his soul, his apostolic work is immense and has produced abundant fruits, others with less merit than he have been canonized and today are part of the spiritual militia of the Church, all of the women kept bustling in and out of the kitchen with refreshments and herb teas, they sought his advice concerning their aches, pains, doubts, had him bless their scapulars and, in swarms, like the Lord's little bees, stored up the fresh dew of his words

like father like son, he says to him, wasn't the calvary that the devil dressed in paper inflicted upon your unfortunate family enough for you?

he is in the jail cell with the prior and half a dozen friars, leaning with them over the pallet of blankets on which he is lying, hunger, suffering and sickness keep him from sitting up, the light trickling through the embrasure is scanty and he tries his best to keep his eyes open so as to make sure that he is not having, as the doctor maintains, yet another nightmare

we have pieced together the papers you tore up, the prior says,

don't you know that obstruction of justice is a crime subject to
very severe punishment? we were looking for your *Treatise on
the Qualities of the Solitary Bird* and have not found it, did you
swallow it whole as witnesses state? have you put it in a safe
place in some monastery of Reformed Carmelites?, thanks to
our missions in lands of infidels and incursions into higher
Ottoman schools of learning we know that the image of the
mystic bird appears frequently in the poetry of the Saracen sect,
a number of heretical books, printed outside our domains,
mention its presence in Kubra, Algazel and Avicenna, unbosom
yourself, tell us straight out, how do you account for these
amazing coincidences?, how did you get access to certain
prohibited works not to be found in our libraries? who
procured them and saw to it that they reached your hands?,
does this subtle, colorless, asexual bird have anything to do
with the ones that the governor of our very faithful island of
Cuba recently had arrested and put in jail in Havana?, what
connection is there between the adepts of the dark night and
that bunch of queer birds nabbed in their nocturnal lairs, whose
execution the public in the stadium is screaming for?
I flew so high, so high, he will finally murmur in a half-faint
the prior, Don Blas and the friars examined with commingled
disdain and rancor the prisoner bundled up in the blankets
were they not there perhaps for the precise purpose of clipping
his wings?

once in the dark of night, when love burned bright with
yearning, o blissful good fortune! I left, how no one knows, my
house already in dull repose, in secret and in rapture, with my
Canticle, disdaining chapels, disavowing nocturnal dens,
seeing in secret signs in the black chambers my delectable Saint
of Saints, o glory of the light-filled night!, Gehenna of the dark
noonday! fearful souls converged toward him along silent,
fecund ways, along bypaths of harsh humors they sought with
me the black light, the circle of pressures and pleasures, the ray
of darkness whereby one knows oneself

go on, go on, he said

(he has a small syringe in his hands

has he just given me an injection? of what medicine or drug?)

I: the one with the thin, endlessly long legs, loose tunic over
filiform extremities, pouches or petticoats with dozens of
dolls, a flowing lilac- or rose-colored cape in which she
wrapped herself as in a flag, had not yet abolished our
kingdom, the Lady, with her bright red mane, fulminated
hieratically in the minibar

does it hurt less now? isn't it true that something like a pleasant
sensation of peace has begun to steal over you?

(was he the one who was speaking or the prior?)

I: we agreed to meet each other there, in the Berber salon with
translucent glass lamps each with a twisted bronze foot, ready
for the journey of the dark night, eager for transcendence and
union, mysteries of pleasure and pain, a fruitful, ecstatic
voyage

tell more, don't stop, I'm all ears!

I: sudden discovery, being simply the rough outer surface,
ignorant of the fiery reality of the Center

we are interested in your version of the black chamber, of what
you did, perceived, heard

I: ardor, ardor, sudden heart palpitations, stirrings and leaps of
the senses, amorous inflammation, ecstasy, consuming love

(the prior, the convulsed face of the prior)

I: going round the circle, hard lashings, shoulders covered with blood, slow psalmody of the Miserere by an invisible choir of friars

don't wander off the subject! our monastic rules do not concern you

I: dissolution, confined space, annihilation of all light, nocturnal voyage, unitive intuition, I am serene, enraptured, enthralled as with a candle he lights a soothing fire in my breast

who?

I: I won't give away names

in the black chamber?

I: on the first night still, in the sensitive antechamber of the abandonment of the senses

did you run into the Archimandrite's familiar, the youngster who was burned at the stake in the stadium?

I: darkness, darkness, delicious secrecy of the inner wine cellar, lurking shadows, delicate touches, gentle cauteries, robust truths, heady wine, ardent passion, fusion, fervent prayer, inexhaustible fountains, fruitful irrigated land, dense and intoxicating virtue, emissions of divine balsam

(they had shaken me up, hit me, pulled on my arm

was my evocation that blasphemous?)

I remained and forgot myself, I say

(they all stare at me, their faces protected by little masks)

I: everything ceased and I left my self behind

doctor, haven't you given him far more than the usual dose of tranquilizers?

on the balconies decorated like theater boxes, porticoes with
coats of arms and aristocratic escutcheons, lavish canvas tents
meant for visitors and relatives, the crème de la crème of the
city, the sweetest honey of the sugar cane, is crowded together
on the journey, ladies with umbelliform or bell-shaped tutelary
hats, panaches of ostrich feathers, tense monocles over an
insolent blue eye, foldable opera glasses with mother-of-pearl
handles, immense flabella that open and close as they fan
themselves with the ostentatious dexterity and swift aloofness
of offended royal peacocks

attracted also by the novelty and color of the spectacle, the
common people stretch out in a line that extends from the
inquisitorial prison to the stadium, heedless of the long wait,
the heat and the flies, apparently absorbed solely in the slow
mastication of lupin and sunflower seeds

(someone has spread the outlandish rumor that they are an
effective remedy against the spread of the plague)

others have managed to get hold of bottles of wine or brandy
and are passing them round, jubilant, bearded, bare-chested
bumpkins, making jokes about us, those handed over to the
secular arm, the cartloads of sick taken to the pyre with all the
pomp and majesty that the circumstances demand, preceded,
surrounded, followed by a cortège of dignitaries, provosts,
oblates, hierarchs of the Order, apostolic commissars, Carmelite Fathers, judges, vicars and scholars from the Holy
Office, the Nuncio with his cope, crosier and ring, a long
procession of deacons and acolytes with sashes and white tunics

(the marquise from the Antilles, in the coachman's seat of her
tilbury and her footman dressed as a marschallin follow
immediately after)

clouds of incense, prayers, drum and bugle corps, chants
drowned out by the uproar of the multitude on seeing the cages,
little portable cells, he says, transported on movable platforms
on which the habituées of the black chamber, of the anxieties
of the dark night, had been symbolically adorned with beaks,

crests, wings and feathers, variegated, exotic birds of a crepuscular visionary geography

> two confessed sinners with black-feathered head, neck and tail, bright red breast and belly, a flowered crest like a bouquet of poppies
> a bird of paradise with tufts of colored feathers on its head and sides, tarred, hairy plumage, tail unfolded like the ribs of a fan
> a horrible barnyard fowl made up like a mask, eyebrows and eyelashes stylized, mascara, rouge, rice powders, lips in the form of a heart tapering into the beak of a booby-bird

the mob was clustered around the cages, their voices drowned out the modulations of terror of a novice modestly disguised as a swallow but, facing the retraction de vehementis or an absurd death, the rest of us accepted the opprobrium inherent in the role with a sort of desperate happiness, allowed ourselves to be carried away by the music, its fanfare began for us the solar gravitation of the ritual, our being put on show with green plumes and a golden sheen filled us with pride, the ominous howl of the crowd in the stadium did not matter to us at all now, the delirious and scandalous appearance of queer birds redeemed us from an existence of humiliation and wretchedness, our most important ambition lay in the perfect identification with the model, that subtle, solitary and ecstatic avian creature that is an allegory for the Sufi soul in Persian engravings and miniatures, we aspired to attain the concise lightness of her flapping wings, the ethereal equilibrium of her steps en pointe, her gentle expression of intoxication at the serene instant of transition, the outsize bird cages had been placed in front of the canopy suspended above the Nuncio, and deliberately apart now from the hubbub and predictable denouement of the proceedings, we pecked at the birdseed, swayed back and forth on the little swings, practiced making our flights smoother, cleaner, more agile, communicated with each other by means of trills and warbles, ending up finding, unintentionally, the ineffable language of the birds

no, that wasn't how it was, let me tell all of you
the Seminarian led the procession, prudently isolated from the others, dressed as a royal peacock, her head crowned with a crest of arborescent structure full of fruits and bunches of grapes, they had put makeup on her to cover up her buboes and sealed her beak with a sort of shield or gag, we were all burning with desire to see her and approach her, her accusations before the authorities had sowed panic in the saunas, fugitives from the one-syllabled long-legged one we fell into the hands of the inquisitors like mosquitoes to end up being roasted to death, encapsulated in her grotesque cage, sprinkled with confetti and covered with paper streamers, she was stewing in the stench of her own slaver, she kept twisting and turning with her odious plumes but they had her securely tied, those carrying her on their shoulders took turns with each other because of the smell and hurried along anxious to see her burned, I followed them panting, not missing a single detail, falling in with the infernal rhythm of their footsteps, I might be recognized and arrested despite my robe, but a curiosity stronger than my fear impelled me to escort her to the stake where she would be fuel for the flames, to witness in ecstasy her convulsions and screams, to insult her, to insult her even as she melted before me into a stinking, scorched heap of matter!

after a long confinement gradually become darker and without hope, he resolved to flee, to escape while still alive from that dungeon in which he was rotting away, to try his luck, to seek refuge in some inn or monastery of his brothers

all he need do was patiently loosen the screw eyes of the padlock, tie and sew together end to end the strips of his blankets torn up in secret, hide the hook of the jailer's oil lamp, await the evening meal and the guards' momentary abandonment of their posts, cautiously force the lock of the door open, stealthily pick his way among the friars sleeping in the corridor, reach the arched window overlooking the cliff above the river, firmly embed the hook between the wood and bricks of the parapet, climb up on top of it and tie to the hook one of the ends of the strips of blanket carefully knotted together, test once more the soundness of his rope, remove his robe and fling it down below, grip the dangling strips of blanket with his knees and hands, slide down to the river-bed gleaming in the moonlight far below, reach the end of his rope and decide, holding his breath, whether to make the blind leap into empty space that would leave his bones on the path around the castle wall or plunge him brutally into the abyss, the waters, the cesspool of Aminadab

bloodthirsty, piercing, inhuman, the shouts and huzzahs from the stadium dimly reached his ears

IV

everything has turned out to be incredibly easy, the official letter of recommendation of the sister group to which he belongs, endorsed and forwarded no doubt by more direct and efficient inner channels, has saved him bothersome paperwork, lightened the burden of formalities, allowed him to bypass the checking of his record by functionaries involved in granting the indispensable permit, that rectangular card with a code number serving as identification and affording access to the kingdom of thought that was erroneous and therefore prohibited, to the accumulation of deviations and presumed revisionist novelties of adversaries, liquidators and renegades, an archive of proofs and documents constituting a written record of the intent, maneuvers, stratagems, delaying tactics of those who in connivance with the enemy through years of intense and pitiless ideological struggle had endeavored to sap the unitary foundations of the mother group, sow dissension and discord, place in doubt the body of doctrine and authority of the commands, conceal beneath seductive appearances of novelty old merchandise long pawed over and unanimously refused, dead sediment left along the riverbank by the impetuous current of history, a prodigious mass of letters, periodicals, documents and works whose harmful nature made the adoption of precautionary measures advisable, requisites such as solid training, indomitable faith, perfect discipline, strict fidelity to the official and correct line on the part of anyone who, for the sound purpose of refuting them and exposing their corrupt falsity, sought permission to go to the sources and drink of their poisonous waters without risk of contagion, a pass, a simple coded pass such as the one that the head librarian handed to him after identifying him and consulting the list of authorized individuals, letting him past with a brusque and brief wave of his arm, gray hair, gray suit, gray general appearance, gaze hidden by the iridescent gleam of light reflected off the lenses of his rimless glasses, it's that way, second door to the left, our interpreter will take charge of

guiding you through the labyrinth of passageways and staircases, the dump heap or burial ground where potentially
contaminating ideas end up requires as is logical certain specific
conditions of secrecy and isolation, he will introduce you to the
attendants and guards on the way to the Gehenna of the attics,
from now on your card will be the open seasame of your visits,
the journey is long and complicated, be patient and don't lose
heart

step after step, stair after stair, he has walked along clinging
like a shadow to the stooped silhouette of the interpreter who
politely moves aside to allow him to go first as they make their
way around the successive obstacles, narrow staircases,
anterooms, iron bars, checkpoints, a long semidark corridor
flanked by dusty mirrors in which he has been able to see
himself reflected full-length before arriving at the little booth
in which the last curator, arrogant and uncivil, is lying in
wait

he has had a look at himself and without the shadow of a doubt
you have recognized yourself

in your wrinkled white summer suit and old-fashioned straw
hat, the romantic sepia print of the young older gentleman

leaning on the windowsill, in profile and with his gaze fixed somewhere outside, he had welcomed me in modest and cordial terms, at first sight the place seems shabby and inhospitable and certain researchers complain for good reason of the insufficiency of the heaters and general absence of conveniences but, even without mentioning the difficult period the country is going through, subjected to economic and ideological siege by an implacable adversary, you will understand that the unprecedented transformation of society which we have embarked upon does not allow us the luxury of allotting this depository of stale theses and inept programs a part of the budget that we desperately need, for the departments of culture and indoctrination, for instance, the physical and mental well-being of millions of ardent and enthusiastic young people, the card catalogues are not always up to date and we lack the computers to which all of you are accustomed but we do our best to compensate for these defects which, as you see, we confess to without the slightest embarrassment, with the warmth and affection of our welcome, the colleagues with whom you will live here for however long your investigations will take are historians who have come from various countries and horizons with the objective of studying and refuting the successive deviations of our infallible doctrine, we have arranged for you to be put up in quarters adjoining the library and you will be served your meals there, our desire is for all of you to take maximum advantage of your stay among us in an atmosphere of seclusion favorable to meditation and study, your having come from contaminated zones and your constant contact with harmful books and materials obliges us to adopt, naturally, a series of prophylactic measures in order to forestall possible contagion, the letters of recommendation of our sister groups are the best guarantee that all of you will be capable of understanding and excusing the rigor of the quarantine, the inevitable irritation of a cordon sanitaire beneficial to everyone, the enfer of the library has a cafeteria and a recreation room, a patio suitable for strolling about inside it at leisure and a place set aside for gymnastics, we cannot offer you the perfection of grand hotels but the service is punctual and painstaking, a team of nurses and doctors will be readily available to you if you fear you have contracted the plague or wish simply to undergo a treatment to detoxify you from poisonous readings, a new concept, more logical and rational, of what scholarly studies and work on the university level ought to be, in the reading rooms you will immediately make new friends and mingle with the other researchers and scholars with study grants, we are, as the saying goes, one big family here

silence, dense, persistent, compact once again as, having seated
yourself at the card catalogue that is to guide you in your
reading of insidious texts, carefully withdrawn from circu-
lation and fallen into a just and lasting oblivion, you observe
out of the corner of your eye the completely quiet, taciturn
involvement of a dozen native inhabitants apparently occupied
in marking with pencils and recording in notebooks whatever
passages of speeches, resolutions, proposals and plenums that
they suspect of alteration or innovation as regards the corpus of
the doctrine

the older gentleman, the obsessive daguerrotype of the still-
young older gentleman, dressed in his wrinkled white suit and
wearing his straw hat despite the current freezing cold, the icy
drafts that filter through windows without weather stripping,
the dirty panes half blurred by fog behind which the snow is
gently falling, was the one image you still retain, yellow, dim
and uncertain after so many years

were you he, as you were sometimes inclined to believe or was it
merely a matter of a double?

the answers of the staff on duty to whom you probably put that
question have not dispelled your doubts

had he really been there, in a place like this, during that
mysterious journey which, in your family circle, was alluded to
only in brief and disapproving whispers?

what confused and disturbed you most was the simultaneous
presence at the school desks of the Kirghiz of indefinable age
dressed in a pair of striped pajamas and the imposing prior of
the monastery accompanied by his familiar

were you not faced once again, as in past visions, with a
flagrant case of anachronism?

the first incursion into the upper shelves of the library with the
help of the parallel bar on the floor to which the iron ladder
was attached offered you an almost incredible accumulation of
vexing surprises, the copies that you are looking for and that
have motivated your long and exhausting journey from the

other end of the continent into the cold prove to have many obliterated fragments, pages ripped out wholesale in a holy access of violence, others carefully stripped of any disquieting idea through an appropriate selection of deletions by scissors, excisions by razors and guillotining by paper cutters

blots and ink stains obscure the comprehension of essential passages, glosses and vituperations of hyena sodomite stinking Jew dirty the clean margins, paragraphs of completely different texts exalting the official line and superhuman virtues of the Leader have been brazenly pasted over the most significant items and articles, a number of volumes have been so badly mutilated as to be illegible and in others the original has been replaced page by page with orthodox doctrinal explanations and trite commentaries, hollow shells bearing the title and name of the author as listed in the card catalogue or padded with material of very different, vulgar content, you are immensely disappointed and as you painstakingly examine the works lined up on the shelves searching for some vestige of the proscribed thought, you contemplate your neighbor in amazement, he too perched, with his fur overcoat and Cossack cap, on a ladder parallel to yours, engrossed in the task of ripping out the last pages of an already ruined volume and exchanging them for others of the same format with an insolence bordering on cynicism, his project of falsification depends as you note on the tolerance if not the support of the director of the library, the attendants on duty collect the extirpated pages in a basket and obsequiously hand up to him from below the ones that are to be substituted for them, how to make him understand that what he is doing constitutes fraud and is an infringement on your basic rights as a researcher?, with grimaces and gestures you try to discredit and throw in his face his serious infraction but the individual does not appear to have the slightest idea of the meaning of your motions and, after removing the binding and tearing up sections of a book that in fact is one of the very ones included on your list of works to be consulted, he hands you with a beatific smile the volume with the new pages that he has just carefully pasted in

the minutes of the last conclave in which, despite the hindrances and pressure brought to bear by the disciplined and docile majority, entirely subservient to the judgment of the Leader, a few sulfurous opponents had taken the floor, have been replaced by old chestnuts from a pompous popular manual of piety!

the investigators in the place appear to have completed the bulk of their work and conceal their compromising inactivity by the almost ritual carrying out of minute tasks, conscientious review of the substituted volumes on the shelves, meticulous checking to make sure that the content of the works labeled in gold letters on the spines of their leather or hardcover bindings in no case matches the title, verification of the fact that the books recorded in the card catalogue do not contaminate with their corrupting ideas the wholesome and peaceable work atmosphere, their long black overcoats and cylindrical hats give them a strange resemblance to dervishes as they go to and from the run-down cafeteria with their teacups, stretch out their numb hands toward the heaters, briefly draw close to the windows of the library and look out on the snow-covered landscape, keep a close watch out of the corner of their eye on the hurried editing of the Kirghiz and the silent, isolated readings of the prior of the Greek monastery and the older gentleman

(was that how it had been? had the journey to the land of his dreams snuffed out his faith through the crudest of processes or cooled his enthusiasm? if not what were the causes of his later aloofness and breaking off of all relations?)

dressed without fail

(it is the one image of him you possess)

in his wrinkled white suit and the straw hat, he has given up the indigestible reading of the text that with infinite and inspiring titles and presentations is to be found in every last one of the rooms of the library and surveys with a gaze full of dismay the melancholy pantheon crammed full of thousands upon thousands of copies of that leaden book

the investigators have left his path to his observation post at the window clear and, with a dreamy air, he presses his still-young face to the glass, only to catch a glimpse of the familiar terrace with its moss-covered balustrade and large pots of hydrangeas, pink clouds, white sails, the incongruous silhouette of an ocean liner whose prow emerges diaphanously from amid the pines, sun like a balloon on fire, shady grove of trees, garden and, in the foreground, the deck chairs and wicker armchairs with imposing backs free of their habitual occupants, identical none the less in his memory to those he contemplated from the balcony at the back of the house

the thermometer placed against the wall, on the little night table full of medicines and clinical equipment, shows the unbelievable temperature of forty degrees centigrade don't pay any attention to them, the Archimandrite says indicating with a slight gesture of his hand the pale and emaciated investigators who are whispering in the shadows, disturbed by the novelty of the conversation we are having, they too are serving a long sentence and know it, otherwise why are they being kept here in quarantine, they too under close surveillance, without the possibility of communicating with their families? their hazardous cleanup work in this contaminating section has exposed them in the eyes of the authorities to contracting the plague and they are treated with the same rigor as the other sick patients, haven't you noticed the precautions taken by the attendants and employees of the cafeteria and their obligatory use of gloves and gauze masks? despite their servility and air of self-importance they are not unaware that their lot is no better than ours, the fur caps and overcoats they bundle themselves up in allow them to conceal attacks of fever and tremors, inner devastation, overwhelmingly virulent symptoms, they cling desperately to the idea that their loyalty to the person of the Leader will suspend their sentence and they will be able to survive in some way or other in this plague-infested area, they are unaware of the implacable logic of the machine that is devouring them, the dilemma of their gradual extinction in the necropolis of the library or the disgraceful exhibition in cages before being handed over to the secular arm and burned at the stake, unlike you and other sympathizers of the same persuasion my extravagant presence in the place did not arouse suspicion, a member of a foreign group and, in their opinion, historically surpassed, my idea of returning to the original source from which certain remote believers in this irrational and superstitious doctrine drank was not, according to their way of looking at things, a threat, they did not know that, by virtue of similar, if not to say identical, situations, created through the transformation of the just aspirations of human beings into a body of powerful and secret dogmas the relation of our mystics to the Church prefigures the one with which to

their misfortune today's so-called liquidators and renegades are
familiar, a Church conceived as an organized congregation of
the faithful and one in which religious power, in spite of its
initial egalitarian intentions, has turned into a superior caste,
isolated from the rest of the believers, unable to agree that all
spiritual values can be contained in a person's individual
conscience, as a few poets and illuminati maintained, without
denying itself or renouncing the immunity and privileges of its
ambitious priestly hierarchy, the conflict between the mystic
experience of the former and the all-powerful ecclesiastical
machinery hence was fated to be resolved through a corpus of
juridical norms destined to lead the recalcitrant to the formal
observance of certain canons or to declare themselves to be in
rebellion against the parish and its iron, intangible unity, as is
said by the author of a little book that never leaves my
possession and has fortunately gone unnoticed by our stolid
cerberuses, if the living have been the object of such brutal acts
one can scarcely imagine what has been wreaked upon the
works of the dead, especially in an era in which the destruction
of a handful of manuscripts could wipe out once and for all the
testimonies of any resistance to the omnipotence and pride of
the hierarchs! didn't you know that, as this deserter from
several Churches whose work I am quoting to you discovered,
the favorite expedient of the orthodox or, more precisely, of
the nucleus of individuals who seize power, has always
consisted of branding each new troublemaker with the mark of
some previously defeated heresy or sect?, in the period in which
the reformer whose poetic brilliance fascinates us lived, it was
not difficult, in order to anathematize the mystics who
disturbed and subverted believers, to skim off some imprudent
phrase written by them and make it coincide with those
delusory and erroneous propositions included in the Edict of
Faith as crimes to be denounced to the Holy Office, an
intangible phalanx of anonymous witnesses accused them of
rejecting prayer and religious ceremonies, sinking into the

ocean of divine love and submerging themselves in passive
contemplation inspired by grace, how could they advocate
without grave danger to their lives the rough road of darkness,
that secluded and secret way of inflamed, naked souls?, the
aridity, the difficulty, the siege of the passion of love, the
anguished feeling of abandonment of the followers of the dark
night and the swooning ecstasies of the black chamber created
scandal, we were creatures doomed to disappear, the harmful
species of a world in which our extermination was a sacred
duty, like those vipers or viscous rats that today display to a
fanatic or frightened populace the spectacle of their deceitful
ignominy, we were forced to accuse ourselves and accuse others
of all sorts of absurd and imaginary crimes, discredited by a
litany of heretical designations, obliged to confess to deviations
and doctrinal poisons which might infect the hale and hearty,
we were to observe the decree which forbade us to meet with
those of our ilk and which closed down the lairs in which we
celebrated our dark secret assemblies and spread our plague
(that black chamber of the sauna that suspended the senses and
in which the mainstay or mooring of our anxieties was kept
intact)
when my familiar wanted to defy the Edict and went out into
the street
the seminarian? I say
yes, don't you know him?
if memory serves me, it was my understanding that
he never leaves my side!
wasn't he burned to death?
the Archimandrite has placed a Philippine cigarette in his
amber cigarette holder, calmly lights it and exhales a mouthful
of smoke before answering in a slightly hoarse voice
you are confused, my friend, the event you mention has not yet
taken place, is it possible that you are not aware that I am
speaking with the still-young older gentleman?

a memory of strolls down the long hallway of the second floor black and white checkerboard floor tiles, period furniture, prints with allegorical subjects, a little statue of the Virgin like an anemic and ailing nymphet enveloped in a purple mantle, portraits of elderly ladies and stern-faced ancestors, summer heat, buzzing of insects, you are in all probability walking about in your bare feet

you are in your uncle's study and you examine the books bound in red and gold lined up on the shelves of the bookcase, history textbooks, collections of works on jurisprudence, popular treatises on medicine and science, manuals of piety, a color print of a pious man, victim of a cowardly assassination by those on the other side, lord and master of that solitary chamber, his entire attention devoted to the scrutiny of your precocious curiosity, a stimulating impulsive itch

you have opened one of the little side compartments of fine handcrafted cabinetwork of the writing desk inside which are piled up cardboard boxes full of photographs, family souvenirs, bundles of letters from long ago and suddenly you come across an image, his image, the older gentleman in a wrinkled white suit and a straw hat whose identity is not yet known to you although his likeness attracts and captivates you

have you guessed, despite your youth, that he is in fact the one who has been proclaimed forever nonexistent, eliminated from the memory of the clan, excluded like a ghostly being from the after-dinner conversations and evocations on the terrace with the moss-covered balustrade and large pots of hydrangeas?, the man without a face whose signs of identity have been blurred, shaded over in a distant dream, blurred and ephemeral?, what secret bond unites the two of you, notwithstanding the hostility of the family circle, capable of summoning you day after day to silent contemplation of him by taking advantage of the moment when the adults read, converse or recite the Holy Rosary in the deck chairs and armchairs with imposing backs set out on the terrace and in the garden?, is he the very one who later will be the hero of your unfinished biography, composed of scattered scraps, like a puzzle with pieces that are lost and cannot be found, didn't the fit of fury remembered by the Archimandrite concerning the destruction of troublesome documents and proofs find blinding confirmation in the annals of your own family?

the older gentleman, the one and only image, already tenuous and nearly vanished, of the older gentleman with his wrinkled white suit and straw hat that was brusquely wrenched from your hands once and for all when, totally absorbed in contemplating it, you failed to notice your uncle's footsteps in the hallway or his silent entrance into the room, surprised while engaged in a shameful and forbidden activity, as ugly and abominable as that of your fateful propensity years later to masturbate yourself with no regard for the distress it caused the Virgin and the fear of eternal punishment

out with you, child!, who gave you permission to poke your nose in my papers and touch what doesn't concern you?

one day the prisoner, on receiving the basket of provisions supposedly sent by his barefoot brothers, thought he glimpsed on the sheet of paper wrapped around the viands the subtle presence of certain veiled handwritten signs

making sure that nobody is spying on him, he has brought the sheet of paper over to the embrasure after heating it with a candle and, like a mirage of water and palm trees amid the austerity of the desert, he has seen verses showing through the paper, carefully traced in pomegranate juice, why do you continue to cling to the earth like a green plant?, are your movements not the key of divine graces?, at the other end of the sheet of paper the heat of the flame also summons, like an incantation, another ardent phrase from Mawlana, our intoxication has no need of wine nor our assembly need of rebecs or harps, neither orchestra or flute, cupbearer or ephebe, we intoxicate and arouse ourselves, drunken creatures that we are!, the message bears the signature Ben Aïds and the prisoner in the monastery of the Carmelite Friars re-uses the paper sent by his colleague to record, also in fruit juice, certain verses of the Canticle for the young and daring professor of Arabic that he is composing in his mind and reciting from memory

from that time on, behind the backs of the guards, the correspondence thus established is enriched with citations from Ibn Al Farid, each time more exalted and bold, we drank in memory of the Beloved a wine that intoxicated us before the creation of the vineyard!, my spirit lost itself in him so perfectly that, without the penetration of one body into another, the two were conjoined in intimate union!, emotion, linked to the secret of that amorous interchange of messages, makes the poet's cruel imprisonment easier to bear, helps him to catch a fleeting glimpse of the delirious Word able to translate, without betraying it, his ineffable experience, wine and not the vineyard, I have Adam for a father, a vineyard and not wine, his mother is my mother, irresistibly attracted him to the ecstasies of Ibn Al Farid and his fiery incoherence, the weekly collations carelessly inspected by those in charge of the refectory of the Order elevate him to the dizzying delirium of an alchemist of language, how to manifest ecstatic states or trances except in a sibylline and ambiguous language, with infinite possible meanings?, they have made distinctions but all is one, our bodies vineyards, our souls wine!

but the pomegranate juice in which the specialist in comparative mysticism has traced the poem turns out on this occasion to be too perceptible and the prior of the monastery discovers, scandalized, the hidden connections between the prisoner and the abominable Islamic illuminati, what meaning to attribute to the verses copied out by Ben Aïds, drink this wine down straight or else mix it with the saliva of the Beloved, any other mixture would be a profanation? do the stations of the dark night not lead to the pleasures and passionate love for which the adepts of gentle cautery feed the flames of the stake amid the roars and huzzahs of the stadium?

ghostly décor of the library, an immense necropolis of books
doomed to annihilation and oblivion, reading rooms plunged
into darkness, windows with meager light opened onto snow-
filled landscapes, heaters that never give out sufficient heat,
dark corridors, cafeteria abandoned by its last suspicious
employees, investigators dressed in long overcoats with the
lapels raised and caps pulled down over their eyebrows,
trembling, pale, emaciated, subject to brusque and violent
attacks of fever, contaminated with the material to the contact
of which they have long been exposed in their self-abnegating
and heroic task of cleaning up, hands covered with gloves with
half-fingers or hidden in their pockets, distrustful of each other
as though on the mutual lookout for the ominous symptoms of
disease, increasingly tottering steps of the sickly-looking one
who suspiciously refuses to shave, contrite vomiting and
diarrhea of the old dean of the Faculty, erythemes and
subcutaneous spots of a laureate awarded a national prize years
before for his eloquent denunciation of Jews who were
spreading the plague, all of them still anxious to go to the
director and the staff to denounce their colleagues' illness, in a
desperate, final attempt at self-serving salvation, without even
tumbling to the fact that those who ordinarily take care of
them and watch over them seem to have disappeared after
disconnecting the call bells and reinforcing the outside locks on
the doors, and so they too are helplessly trapped, like the
foreign visitors, inside the accursed net

> the Kirghiz of indefinable age dressed in striped pajamas
> who hands out little pieces of paper with the words
> becquerel rays, millirads, radioactive isotopes, iodine
> 131, strontium, ruthenium, cesium written in four
> different alphabets
> the Archimandrite, heavily made up, opulent, cope edged
> in feathers, miter with the plumes of a cuirassier, crosier
> turned into a scepter

the Seminarian with the bold tongue and the outlandish
pink garters

all the habitués of the library made of cardboard stage flats and
fake bookshelves reduced to miniaturized figures of stage or
screen contemplated from the head of a sickbed
I or the older gentleman?

his inclusion among the condemned, he says, was the fruit of
sheer chance, they were looking for a suitable place in which to
shelter him and help him complete his work in a noble and
well-meaning effort to compensate for the unfortunate effects
of the catastrophe through a meticulous and patient labor of
rescuing the memory and culture of that entire people suddenly
swept away, the accident, as you know, spread its skullcap of
radioactive cloud in a matter of hours over the whole of the
territory, luckily sparsely populated, in which his countrymen
carried on their nomadic way of life, it was not simply fate but
human error and, above all, the product of lack of foresight and
carelessness as the investigating commission established beyond
all possibility of doubt on drawing up the list of infractions of
the rules and lack of patriotic discipline of those who were
unjustly excluded from the organization and subject to the
jurisdiction of special tribunals, the worldwide repercussions
of the tragedy tarnishing the reputation and good name of our
country forced us not only to adopt extremely severe measures
to prevent contamination of other areas but also to create
humanitarian commissions to settle particularly dramatic cases
such as that of the chance survivor to whom you, in your verbal
obfuscations and deliriums, frequently referred, that individual
of indefinable age in striped pajamas, for whom a place has
been found among his peers thanks to official advice and
protection in order for him to undertake the invaluable
compilation of the language, past, legends, customs and
history of the destroyed community, no place better than the
library, with all the resources of science at his disposal, he could
facilitate his solitary labor in a stimulating atmosphere of
sympathy, cordiality and understanding
is he talking, talking still, bending down toward him with his
rimless eyeglasses, with clear and sometimes gleaming lenses?
(he has a hypodermic syringe in his gloved hands and gradually
inserts in it the reddish-colored contents of a small glass
capsule)

now that my collaborator has gone away and no one can hear
us I will speak frankly, the Kirghiz held captive with the others
in the library, witness of the tragedy that befell his brothers of
the sub-Arctic forest has turned out to be disloyal to his
sponsors by wreaking subtle and secret vengeance on them
he: do I have a fever?
the usual one, a few tenths of a degree, don't move
he: I can barely hear your voice
I'm sorry, did I hurt you?
(divine glow, inner illumination, uncreated light, spiritual
must, heat of wine in the veins, drenching, ecstatic intoxication)
in the act of rescuing the heritage of his dead for the benefit of
those who caused the extermination, he chose to invent starting
with semantics a colossal imposture assigning an arbitrary
meaning to the words that he is checking and events that he is
classifying, just as some twenty centuries before, in very similar
circumstances of anguish and cultural loneliness, another faker
of genius contrived a gratuitous pairing of the hieroglyphic
signs and the Greek and demotic texts of a stone world-
renowned today, entirely succeeding in his aim of deceiving
everybody, haven't you seen, don't you see how he appears to
be having a most enjoyable time and is laughing to himself as
he makes up whimsical terms and designations to confuse
specialists and make fools of them? the memory of how much
was taken away from him in that frightful accident belongs to
him alone and he is unwilling to share it with anyone, look
how amid the emaciated, sick, ideologically irradiated investigators, he grows younger and younger and glows with a
sort of happiness!, the historical fraud he is perpetrating with
the painstaking care and patience of an ant helps him to survive
in a world that has no direction and no incentives, only
mordant laughter, incomprehensible to those round about him
who take him for a nut, comforts him in his undertaking,
nobody is in on the truth of his killingly funny legacy and I beg

you to be discreet, the slightest allusion or mention on your part to my assistants and nurses in the course of your cycles of fever and oneiric visions could be used against me and against him, don't betray the confidence I am rashly sharing with you, times are hard and the best way to go on living is to know when to seal one's lips cross section of the library seen as an aquarium, a thousand-year deposit of manuscripts reduced to a sort of mire in which flashy aquatic species, seaweed, sargassum, blue-green algae, jellyfish with snaky locks, currents of oxygen supplied by tubes, inner lighting hidden by arborescences of coral or madrepore, iridescent streams of perfect bubbles, schools of transparent fishlets and tail fins of alarming brightness have established themselves

the native investigators are still there in their overcoats and caps, forsaken, squalid, waxen, slimy hands and noses glued to the glass, mouths grown fleshless from the syndrome desperately exhale little globules of air, heavy black frock coats give them the grotesque appearnace of polar birds, with fragile yellow finger joints they test in vain the solidity of the glass that imprisons them as though they were trying to beg for help or arouse the pity of those passing by

(have they been irradiated, suffered the inner devastation of the plague, are they dying of asphyxiation in that phosphorescent maritime prison?) you walk on, I walk on, overcome by a subtle feeling of weightlessness, of floating gently like the little fish in the aquarium of ferns and algae, emanations of steam and damp spots on greenish oozing walls indicate that I am approaching the hot rooms, the series of vaulted chambers in which the devotees of the public baths perspire tightly girdled in their shrouds, light from directly overhead, dense hazy atmosphere, blurred silhouettes and faces, panting figures in togas, lovers who emerge from the fog, their undergarments patently jutting out, elusive vestals with tiny nylon panties, I remain face downward in the state of supersensitive receptivity that precedes the ritual ablutions and immersion in the waters of the pool, moments of fruitful somnolence and perceptive intellection, the prelude or antechamber of the abandonment of the senses, gradual ascesis to the abysses of delight of the saint, inner night of confinement and darkness, black chamber of our outpourings and ecstatic rapture

don't stop, he says, the scribe is taking down everything
(who is speaking?, do they want to worm out of him with
drugs and deception what they have not managed to get from
him with threats and blows?, is it still the Carmelite prior or is
it Don Blas in person?)
the music, the music of the piano coming from down below,
the Berber salon with translucent glass lamps each with a
twisted bronze foot in which the Lady sadly tells her notes one
by one in possession once again of her amazon's wig, the fiery
splendor of her mane
(is it the melody that she played when as a lonely, plague-
infested widow, fleeing from the recriminatory presence of the
family, she shut herself up in the salon in the lower depths of the
house in search of a pleasant and protective zone of shadow?)
you do not know nor can you know, engrossed, all ears in the
musical execution of the piece whose score you know by heart,
a piano mysteriously transported to the now-destroyed favorite
spot of the Lady, a grand salon with side benches covered in
worn red oilcloth, Second Empire gas lamps, wall frescoes of
Near Eastern landscapes, green hills, horsemen, silhouettes of
burnooses and haiques, little hermitages with white cupolas,
spiky minaret of a mosque, a snow-white crescent moon
as you lie face down still on the hot marble floor tiles,
fascinated by the gradual insinuation of the tender, captivating
melody, she is alone in her hiding place and I know I must not
interrupt her, merely prick up my ears and accompany her in
spirit as she flees from the asphyxiating severity of destiny,
dishonor of a union not blessed by God and struck by the
lightning of His holy wrath, opprobrium of a lineage forever
tainted by her union with a heretic, a nature permanently
stigmatized whose sambenito, the garment of one publicly
shamed by the Inquisition, will be hung on the walls of
churches as a warning and a subject of scandal for future
generations
happiness, well-being, beatitude, close fusion with a music

that drives away the clouds hiding her, her silhouette of a young widow clinging to the piano that is the consolation for her misfortunes, luminous reconstruction of memory in the much-missed salon of the Lady, improvised auditorium in which habitués, husky suitors, novices listen enthralled to the Sonata, bathed in sweat, trembling with fever or emotion, forehead resting on the marble tile, suddenly anxious to get to your feet and abandon the vault in which you are lying like a dead body enveloped in the folds of its shroud, at the beginning of the Sufi dance, whirlwind of souls in thrall to the universal force of solar gravitation, mystic fire of the sama?, the singers modulate their diaphanous voices, the dervishes spin like toy tops, their drunken round attains the grace of levitation!, are they perhaps chanting the verses of Ibn Al Farid and Mawlana that Ben Aïds has smuggled into your cell written in pomegranate juice?

and all of a sudden

stabbing pains, flutes out of tune, broken violins, discordant and inharmonious sounds, screeching stringed instruments, hurrying footsteps, closed piano cover, music that grows faint and dies away

doctor, I swear to you that this is unbearable!

your outcry was heard amid the confusion of insane movements, hysterical screams, flight of terrified insects, high-pitched voices crying out it's come, it's come, our turn has come, she's melted the mistress's buttocks and brain, we can do nothing against her or her evil shadow, her piercing look emits a deadly wave of radiation, will it take her more than a few seconds to make complete wrecks of us?

relapsed into a dream state, fungous unreality, contained anxiety, apprehension regarding the meeting that foreseeably awaits you, fruitless attempts to get up out of bed, leave the room, flee from this fake hospital with all the hallmarks of a psychiatric prison, dull pain, inner corrosion, secret torment, tossing and turning in bed, uncontainable agitation, ominous presentiment of the inevitable approach of danger, uncontrollable gestures of terror, imminence of the apparition that you most fear magnetized by the violence of your own panic, you see it, you now see it, the grotesque figure of the sower of discord with the one-syllable name, the big clumsy clogs on the last step of the staircase, incredibly long legs, loose tunic above filiform extremities, handbag or petticoat with dozens of dolls, long dark plaited locks, vast tutelary hat whose wide brim appears to summon forth the flight of a flock of crows, caught like a moth in the circle of an intense summer light as, after flinging the little figures onto the floor and witnessing the agony of the victims with sovereign impassibility, it hones to a fine point its pupils hidden in the blackness of its veils, purifies the incandescence of their coals, holds out for endless seconds her witch's index finger and brusquely unleashes upon me the siege, the waters, the cavalry of Aminadab

had he drowned to death, plunged into the spiral of the
whirlpool, drawn into the maelstrom of the abyss by the
torrential force of the waters?

a clear sensation of asphyxia and the awareness of having
struggled in vain against the irresistible suction that was
swallowing him up lent support to the thesis of the fall, of his
having been sucked up by the evacuatory vortex of the sewers

had someone, there above, simply pressed a lever, activating the
flush of water and his descent into the bowels of the earth
enveloped in the spirals of the maelstrom?

like those cockroaches flies or ants lodged in the toilet bowl
that we examine briefly, with dim satisfaction, before un-
leashing the mechanism that puts an end to their parasitical
existence, had he been contemplated in turn by the omnipotent
and unknown executor of another sentence equally hazardous
and admitting of no appeal?

who, how, why?

no answer or explanation, only the recollection of his
suffocation, immersion, desperate search for air

V

once again the terrace overlooking the sea with the moss-covered balustrade and large pots of hydrangeas, the serene, hot late afternoon without the relief of an occasional breeze
they are seated in a semicircle in half a dozen wicker armchairs with imposing backs, next to the ancient arbor decked with wild grapevines, in the lacy shadow of the acacias
(with your back to the sea since you are looking directly at them settled stiffly in their chairs, as on a stage set)
a woman with a red beret and an angular, withered face, a thickset blonde, an uncle with motorcycle goggles like horse blinkers, a stern-faced aunt dressed in mourning, two lady refugees from the neighborhood who are difficult to identify bathed in the splendid aura of the imminent sunset, the apotheosis of pastel pink tones in the distant background of the tableau which they constitute, dressed in the autumnal elegance that the scene demands, actors and extras in an exhaustively rehearsed performance, absorbed in the mimicry and the playing of their roles, requisite references to the Uprising, crusade of national salvation, values of the race, heroic deeds and exploits, fertilizing blood of martyrs, fatherland recovered at last, evocation of crimes and abominations of the adversary, mobs, arson, Red secret police, priests and nuns murdered in the most cowardly way, the emotional voice of Doña Urraca, widow of an early martyr to the Cause and adoptive wartime godmother, moving anecdotes of the bravery of our Moroccan troops, miracles of faith, examples of virtue and ferocity, evidence of heaven's aid to the Cause, compassionate allusions to her, an unmarried mother with a son, victim of her own immaturity and thoughtlessness, isolated from the world after her disgrace, marked forever by the stigma of a condemned union, an unholy civil marriage, Republican-style cohabitation, an indelible stain on the good name of the family, its spirits crushed by the force of the blow, logical and just end of that declared enemy of God and country, fleeing from herself and her family, deprived of the use of

reason, inwardly devastated by the torrential flood of her illusions and hopes, a defenseless creature without means dependent on the charity of relatives, incapable of looking after the little boy, sweet-tempered, mercifully estranged from the world, except for music, the piano, the melancholy notes of the piano, the daily execution of obsessive melodies, happy in her own way during the interpretation of the Sonata, she has varied her repertory as though her need to return to it were less obsessive than on other afternoons, poor thing, do you hear her?, it's a more lively march, we used to play it two-handed at parties and benefit recitals, she was pious and happy in those days, who would ever have guessed what destiny had in store for her?, words, bits and pieces of sentences that reach his ears, those of the little boy playing in the grass in front of the stage set lighted by a big round red sun, the semicircle of shell-shaped wicker chairs, the table with the tray of drinks, the familiar ritual of fanning, gestures of dejection, sighs of nostalgia, perpetual afternoon whose fiction tints with mocking rosiness the barren décor of the terrace is the memory of a memory of a memory still a memory?

from the balcony, grasping the railing of the balcony on the front façade of the house he observes the adults bustling back and forth with wooden crates and cardboard boxes full of unwholesome works, our troops have just entered the town, berets shirts bandoliers boots, a rough tide of upraised arms, hymns, speeches, triple hoarse invocation of the charismatic savior, public session of purification and exorcism, ashen light and the acrid smell of burning, corrupt manuscripts thrown into the fire, scandal sheets with strange indecent figures, the devil dressed in paper, obscene caricatures of the King and the Pope, contaminating writings of Jews Marxists Freemasons atheists inspected pro forma without the culpable indulgence of the curate and the barber, everything must disappear without a trace, dangerous ideas, perverse utopias, suspect promises meant to trap and poison unwary souls, let them act with holy intransigence without a single exception, even books seemingly harmless at first glance may contain within them insidious proposals cunningly disguised, we must sweep our soil clean of all filth and impurity, God is with us and approves with satisfaction this robust affirmation of patriotic Christian faith

pages and more pages of fine print blackened, twisted, convulsed, like the souls of their authors in Hell Don Blas says, done away with by the fervent zeal of the guardians of orthodoxy amid cries of joy, hurrahs, applause, Deo gratias, the entire population out on the streets to witness the ceremony of expiation, the procession of the hierarchs of the Order, Fathers of Mount Carmel, Inspector General at the front of the Calced Friars, offerings and vows to the Virgin, the anemic and ailing nymphet borne about on a portable platform, blowing of bugles, beating of drums, resurrected royal purples, rain of roses, slow movement forward, rhythmic march

from the balcony, with your head leaning on the grating of the railing, you contemplated, you contemplate, scattered by the

wind like dried thistle flowers, the embers and ashes of the
library of the older gentleman now executed by a firing squad

I visited a house in which it was my duty to perform a work of charity, the entrance was gloomy, dirty and full of spider webs, the brick flooring was badly cracked, three broken-down chairs and a sagging bed were all the furniture there was in that narrow little room in which lived an emaciated woman crushed by the weight of her misfortune

alms, help, administration of one of the sacraments of our Holy Mother Church?

no, the letter of a man condemned to death by our exceptional tribunals, a few lines of farewell written in the chapel by the criminal after learning of his sentence

the husband?

father of her son and responsible for her troubles, a union not blessed by God

her?

yes, clasping the child without saying a word as I handed her the message from the man who had ruined her life with illusory and impious ideas, from the one who had brought the devil dressed in paper into that upright house

a Red?

worse than that!, even his fellows deemed his doctrines to be subversive and heretical and excluded him from their organization, when we arrived he was hiding from them and their secret services, concealed in a dank cellar so as to save his skin

did he repent?

no, his heart was hardened by pride and he refused to accept spiritual aid, I tried in vain to soften that lump of solid lava by enumerating the misfortunes that his lack of belief and stubborn persistence in evil had entailed, God had blinded his eyes and stopped up his ears, he refused to make confession maintaining that he was at peace with himself and the only thing he asked of me was to do him the favor of transmitting a letter to the abandoned mother of the orphan

did you investigate its contents?

yes, I read it, motivated by the ardent hope that in it he would bare his soul, admit that he had been led inexorably into a blind alley by his credo, his rebellion against any and every natural form of control and authority

wasn't that what happened?

not at all! his will and testament exhorted her to bear her trials with stoicism and remake her life but he did not even call upon God's infinite mercy!

what was her reaction?

she held the child tightly in her arms without a single lament, her eyes were dry, she looked my way without seeing me, as though she did not understand what was happening or the tenor of the letter, suddenly, permanently, irremediably deprived of the faculty of reason

(was the scene imaginary or real?, that of the funereal painting, dirty and full of spider webs placed onstage in the harsh and violent light of the electric bulbs by Don Blas and the mute, frail woman with a celluloid doll in her lap, weren't they part of a performance of *The Devil Dressed in Paper* in the school run by the Fathers which he had attended years before?)

the ladies in the orchestra seats remained engrossed in contemplation of the edifying spectacle, approving the chaplain's speeches with emphatic gestures and vigorous nods of their heads, feeling sorry for the misfortunes of the woman clutching the boy doll, exchanging helpful comments on the weather and the insidious radioactivity of the environment, the deadly plague that was decimating the black chambers and their devotees of the dark night, those exotic creatures exhibited in cages disguised as birds before being taken off to the stake amid the shouts and hurrahs of the stadium, they whispered and pointed a finger at the one in the plumed hat and long gloves with her neck and breastbone covered with a silk shawl, with dark circles under her eyes, gaunt, wasted, shaking with fever, who furtively vomited into her handkerchief and ominously displayed all the symptoms of the disease she had gone out to take a breathing spell, get a bit of night air, discover the destiny and vicissitudes of other decent families, as many as had survived in hiding or managed to find asylum inside some embassy, mobs were setting fire to churches, holy images were being destroyed, corpses of priests who had been shot lay on the sidewalks, the atmosphere was filled with smoke, it had become unbreathable, at home we were hiding two little cloistered nuns and I was carrying in my handbag, clutching it to my breast, a small box of consecrated holy wafers that a pious soul had managed to save from the tabernacle before the rabble burst into the parish church, flung the holy monstrance onto the floor and stamped on it in fury, the whole neighborhood had a hostile and phantasmagorial look about it, a sharp, tenacious, clinging smell of pesticide or burnt flesh hovered about chapels and temples, the militiamen had set up checkpoints and were subjecting decent people to a rough and humiliating search, the discovery of a prayer book or missal, of a rosary or religious print could lead to a severe sentence with no appeal possible, I cautiously continued on my way, hidden in the shadow and fearful of being detected, clutching to my bosom, poor little me, the small box of Sacred Forms the discovery of which would have aroused the fury of that lawless horde, well-off and respectable persons appeared to have vanished, replaced by old hags of the lower classes and individuals who looked like gallows birds, hey señora, where are you going with such a mysterious air and in such a hurry?, could you by any chance have in your handbag a divine gold ciborium full of consecrated hosts?, they were guffawing at me with crass gestures and rude looks, they were ridiculing the aristocratic exquisiteness of my attire, a lilac-colored organdy outfit with lace veils and big bows, bead necklaces, medals and cameos, white silk stockings, high-heeled shoes with rhine-stone buckles and fake jewels at the instep, I stealthily slithered past them, my movements were those of a sleepwalker, despite the protection of my makeup applied with care, my face was beaded with sweat and I wiped it with a hanky, my figure stood out against the ashen background of pathetic twilight fog, an old-fashioned lady of the Right inflamed by the closeness to The One I was sheltering within my breast, a devotee of kindled passion and fusion of sensitive and pure souls, eagerness for transcendence and union, mysteries of pleasure and pain, ecstatic fruitful voyage, incapable of reacting in the face of the grave danger that threatened, patrol of the streets by residents of the neighborhood on the lookout for those infected with the plague, general roundup of suspects, immediate closing of black chambers and dens of bliss, obligatory appearance before the health authorities so as to be subjected to blood tests and discover those who bore the virus, removal of those who were sick in carts and cages to the stadium where they would perish at the stake, I had managed to bribe the director of a hospital to certify that my blood was pure, free of any sort of bad mixture or taint, a document testifying to my noble Christian lineage going back generations on all four sides but the hoax had been spotted by the vicars of the General Inquisitor and the inspectors proceeded to verifications in situ with computers directly connected to the data of the blood bank, my certificate that cost me a bundle was worthless and I found myself liable to be denounced by the informers snooping around the neighborhood, was I Jewish?, was I a mystic?, did I belong to the guild of those drowned in divine love?, of devotees of the ray of darkness and abysses of delight of the saint?, passers-by whose path I crossed hurried quickly on with hatred and fear painted on their faces, hey, you, the one with the feather duster, why are you walking in the dark so close to the walls?, come into the light so we can see you!, have you passed the blood tests required by law, show us the certificate, if you've got one!, a group of four, with the uniform and boots of the Party, had surrounded me, they had flashlights in their hands and were looking for the telltale symptoms of the disease on my neck, face and extremities they: why are you covering up your neck and throat with so many bows and all that lace?, may we take your temperature and palpate your groin and armpits?

I: my health is absolutely perfect! I have a printed document with an official stamp and the signature of the hospital doctor, I have as well, I have in addition

they: if you have as many proofs of your purity as you say, why did you try to sneak away and why are you trembling so?

I: I was bringing aid to a friend's house, a charitable deed for a person who is helpless, old, and destitute

they: somebody who's plague-ridden, like you are!

I: I swear to you that

they: do you have the zero-negative certificate or don't you?

I: I was in such a rush to be off that I left it at home but I promise you that

they: don't you know that by law you are required to show it whenever the authorities ask to see it?

I: I know, I know, I forgot, let me go back home and I'll bring it to you right away

they: we could give you the test right now in our mobile unit but since my buddies and I are in a good mood we'll authorize you to go on to your friend's house if you play ball with us

I: what do you want from me?

they: the money you've got in that handbag, tomorrow's a holiday and partying with some honest to goodness women would suit us fine, just have a good time and a few drinks together, we're doing you a favor, cutie!

I: take whatever you like!

they: don't be scared, dearie, and keep a sharper eye out from now on, two blocks farther on there's another patrol and you might find them less accommodating, so if you want my advice you'd best put some distance between you and them and get the hell out of here

I: thanks, a thousand thanks!

they divided up the packets of bills between them by the light of the flashlights and I wandered on aimlessly, in a state of hallucination from the scenes of pillage and arson, recriminating wall posters, buildings shut down, slogans vomited out through the loudspeakers of the Neighborhood Association of Upright Citizens, an excited crowd seemed to be running after me, orders voices barks grew louder and louder, informers had perhaps done their job and the pack was seeking its prey in the dead-end streets of the neighborhood, my pursuers, I saw, were wearing rubber gloves and gauze masks to guard against contagion, I fled from them struggling against the unleashed fury of the wind whipping the plumage and veils of my hat and sensed their cries, exclamations, panting breath coming closer and closer, what were they going to do to me?, put me in a cage?, parade me through the streets like a trophy?, do me in once and for all with a sudden burst of their pesticides?, herd me into the stadium with the others who'd been irradiated? hermetic faces, oxidized by the saline corrosiveness of the air passed by me one after the other like an endless traveling shot, everything contributed to putting obstacles in my way in this unequal race, the stiletto heels of my pumps got twisted, I had lost my sense of direction and had no idea where my steps were taking me

(the ladies grouped in the semicircle of deck chairs and wicker armchairs with imposing backs remain gravely and attentively silent, the leaves of the hydrangeas are misleadingly still, not one little bird peeps from the tops of the acacias)

hanging on tight to my handbag, with the little box full of Sacred Forms, I managed to take refuge in the house of a Catholic family where a priest who had escaped from the mob gave us all communion isolated from the world, inside a plastic bubble, I spied on the neat and tidy room of that prison hospital with its organization charts and medical equipment, the nurse with hands sheathed in gloves, the little table on wheels with disposable syringes and flasks of serum, I wanted to have a few words with the staff but the protective membrane of their immunological systems stifled the sound of my words, I moved my lips without producing the slightest sound, I tried to keep my eyes open and contemplated the miniaturized garden on the television screen, a balustraded terrace with views onto the sea and large pots of hydrangeas, shell-shaped wicker armchairs, pink clouds in the late afternoon, motionless acacias, apparently stagnant air, flutter of fans, sighs, barely whispered phrases, a group of highborn ladies absorbed in incessant and incomprehensible conversation, no doubt a reconstruction of adventures and incidents, moments of bliss and splendor described with that painstaking care and desire for precision of detail that exile demands, scrupulous fidelity to the rites of the world that has disappeared, hands of the dial stopped at an unlucky date

did they speak of the redeeming Crusade, hardships, martydoms, recent communiqués announcing victory, the inexorable advance of their side, outrages and crimes of the rabble?, of the havoc caused by the cruel visit of the ugly bird to the Lady's temple of love?

did they listen to the piano, the melodic notes of the piano, the Sonata interpreted by her, muffled, remote, almost inaudible through the protective membrane of the bubble?

was she playing, playing expressly for me?

I want to hear her, let me out of here this minute!

(had the outcry died in my throat or had they carried their severity to the point of pretending to ignore it?)

I saw her, I saw her none the less, in her sound and light show, the most delicate luminous and acoustic images, I climbed toward her and the multiform brilliance and sparkle of the

whites dazzled my eyes at each new stage of the ascent, a
knowing virtue illuminated and purified her features with the
greater intensity of the splendor of each of the successive
circular spheres

nocturnal journey of the prophet?, secret ladder of the saint?,
unreal, radiant, diaphanous bridge?

her face was of living flame

had the author of the Canticle endeavored to disguise his inflamed passion, ecstasy and flights of rapture with a veil of theology and soothing, gentle commentaries with the intention of avoiding the anathema of the Holy Office and the obtuse bloodthirstiness of the Unreformed Carmelite Friars?, or was he perhaps trying to condense and compound to the utmost the enigma of his verses by surrounding them with a halo of ambiguity and mystery impossible to pierce?, what correlation could in fact be established between the effect of the "from the inner wine cellar of my Beloved I drank" and the glosses that instead of shedding light on its sense following an orthodox interpretation envelop it in a complex hermeneutical net at once redundant and contradictory?, do not the touch of a spark, mellow wine, emanations of divine balsam, as explained by the reformer, perhaps refer to a universe of irremediable imprecision of language in which each word takes on an aleatory plurality of meanings?

Ben Aïds brings with him the codex to the *Praise of Wine* and points with his finger to the sibylline verse of Ibn Al Farid paraphrased in a number of divergent ways by his exegetes, one saying wine really means that there is no other God but God and saliva is Mohammed the prophet of God, and another that if you mix true existence (wine) with the forms of perishable things, you must not abandon The One you love, for the Beloved's vital sap (saliva) comes directly from that!

(how did he manage to get to his room? weren't visits, even by the immediate family, strictly forbidden? has he gotten the better of the collective terror of contagion or did it infect him as well?) they said, by drinking it you have sinned but in all truth I have tasted only that of which I would have been guilty of depriving myself! (are the words of Ben Aïds verses of Ibn Al Farid or do they reproduce in an incomprehensible form hidden sentiments that are his and his alone?)

the cell is empty once again, a hole some six feet wide and ten feet long hollowed out in the wall of stone, with a single niggardly embrasure that gives onto the half-shadow of the corridor

a bed of planks, a torn dirty blanket, an earthenware bowl full of ashes, a sheepskin that does not even reach down to his knees, cold, shivers, convulsions, fever

is he talking, still talking?

I come from a people who, when they love, die

the Lady, they say, don't you remember her?

you first met her in the convent in the Sierra, she was one of
those blessed persons with just a bit of the bawd, of a Celestina,
about her, who by dint of false syllogisms and only half-
understood theologies firmly state that they are following the
supposed via unitiva of perfect souls, seek a reputation for
sanctity and claim for themselves all sorts of miracles, stigmata
and states of ecstasy, she maintained that in order to calm the
soul and rid the heart of every human thought fervent ecstasy
and the complete abandonment of the senses must be attained,
stated with assurance that one could in no way predict the
tyrannical movements of the body and on this pretext
abandoned herself to a plethora of libidinous and depraved
impulses without thereby losing one iota of her innocence, the
friend of deluded confessors and wandering friars, she lived
surrounded by a horde of them and encouraged them to self-
abandonment and contemplation accompanied by their
touching and manipulating of themselves until palpable and
crude movements of the senses were produced, burning passion,
sweating, fainting spells, melting in the love of God, to the
great scandal of pious and right-thinking minds, she, the Lady,
told whoever was willing to listen to her, and there have been
many who were dumb enough to be taken in, that since the age
of seven, she had been secretly courted by a handsome youth to
whom she was betrothed and with whom she lived conjugally,
a fact that she revealed to no one because he was the Beloved,
who since that time had favored her with fits of ecstasy, visions
and the enjoyment of a perpetual chastity impossible to
blemish, although she had been known as Francisca before,
when she arrived at the convent and you gave her confession she
had everybody call her la Calancha, whatever she told you
under the priestly vow of secrecy you took as the truth and she
revealed to us when subjected to torture that you encouraged
her to continue to follow the loving path of thirsty souls

as you composed and recited your esoteric poem and gave

yourself over to the Ottoman levitation dance, our fervent custodians of law and order tried her and she appeared at a public auto-da-fé with a black candle in her hand, flogged through the streets and squares in punishment and scorn for her conspiracies and her abominable commerce!

harried, exposed to the wrath of the populace, she fled the country to escape her disgrace and, after using her mature charms on the Saracens, she found herself a place in the Luciferous shadow of Voltaire in a den with waters, airs, nocturnal ardors and fears in which, in the black chamber of their accesses of rapture and salacious acts, the devotees of the dark night descended to the deep caverns of sensation, drank the heady, heavy wine of infidels dripping their substance, or can it be that you no longer remember your own verses?

the Lady, yes the Lady, from whom you regularly bought a ticket for sixty-five francs so as to enter her impure and filthy apartments with the other odd birds, an old woman, a very old woman, however hard she tried to hide that fact with makeup and girlish ways, artificially rejuvenated by facial operations, wigs and porcelain dentures, clinging to her faded aristocratic image, proudly erect, hieratic, surprised on her little throne in the minibar by the outbreak of the plague, struck down by the index finger of the grotesque figure in the apotheosis of her discreet and subterranean kingdom with her pure white dental prosthesis and flaming orange hair!

why did they delay with all sorts of subterfuges, procrasti-
nations and evasions handing over the mirror that I kept asking
for so insistently?, were they afraid that the sight of my gaunt
face, wasted away by the dampness and dimness of the cell,
emaciated by the fasts and the miserable prison diet would
betray the excesses of cruelty that they wreaked on me and
endorse the words of Mother Teresa who would rather have
seen me in Moorish territory than in the hands of those who
treated me with such ferocious rage and brutality?, the skeletal
withered hands that stuck out from the long sleeves of the
odious straitjacket looked like the talons of a bird of prey, my
skinny rib cage threatened to collapse and break in response to
my persistent efforts to stand upright, my thin back plagued me
without respite after so many floggings and lashings, my knees
barely held me up when, dragged to the church to recite the
Miserere, I was obliged to put up with their threats and insults
in a kneeling position, a sanctimonious and presumptuous
ordinary monk who put on the airs of a poet and scholar and in
truth was ignorant, vainglorious and dull-witted, hardened in
error, made arrogant by dreams of grandeur, deaf to the
decisions of the monastic chapter and decrees of the Apostolic
Nuncio!
they collected in a crowd at the door of the dungeon, chatting
with the bailiffs or the turnbox monk, spying through the
peephole and commenting on my slightest gesture, just look
how he keeps moving his lips, he's reciting his verses under his
breath so as to memorize them, he doesn't want to write them
down because he's afraid we'll get hold of them and discover
their bizarre and fallacious content, he's delirious because of
the opiates the doctor makes him take and he confuses his
temporary periods of calm with divine illuminations and
ecstatic states of rapture, his body is nothing but a heap of
bones, he's no more than a shadow now and no miraculous
remedy can restore him, he's entered the terminal phase of the
illness and his face and extremities are covered with buboes and

rashes, no nurse wants to come anywhere near him even with mask and gloves on, his organism is decomposing while he's still alive, a soft, shapeless mass impregnated with humors lies all around him there between the sheets, he's in his death throes, don't you see?, his sight is clouding over, the plague is slowly eating him away, devoured, dissolved, melted away, a horrifying vestige of his former self, a real human wreck

our life was a game of Russian roulette, she says as she lights a
Philippine cigarette with trembling hands and recomposes her
devastated face as best she can, every fortuitous meeting in
woods and thickets with no other law or function save for that
love now become our only exercise, each visit to the kingdom
of darkness that extinguishes the torments of the flame that
consumes and yet causes no pain turned into an ordeal, might
not the Beloved from whose wine cellar we drank and whom
we abandoned satiated with his delightful knowledge be the
instrument chosen by destiny to annihilate us, the seductive
disguise of the executioner chosen by the accursed apparition
with the one-syllable name to carry out her sentence?, how
many times, in the arms that I love best, I repeated to myself
the verses of the Sufi master of Ben Aïds, my heart says that you
are my ruin, may my soul be your redemption whether you
know it or not!, and once the thin membranes of such a sweet
encounter had been broken, we returned to our hideouts in
terror, had ill fortune touched us?, were we contaminated
without knowing it?, was the source of contagion already in
our blood?, the grotesque figure had begun its death-dealing
incursions by way of the temple of the devotees and from there
spread its havoc like a train of gunpowder, the guard of the
mine shaft where those adepts eager to experience pressures and
pleasures were in the habit of intertwining their limbs till they
formed a single cluster, encountered early one morning a dense
and worrisome silence and, from stairway to stairway, tunnel
to tunnel, chamber to chamber, witnessed the spectacle of the
Gehenna, no longer that of seas of light darkness fire water
snow and ice, but that of cadaver after cadaver manacled, their
feet and necks shackled, chained to each other, hung up on
butcher's hooks, immobilized forever in their ecstasies by the
threatening index finger of the ugly bird

what to do? she says, decked out in all her Archimandrite's
finery, after just slightly retouching the outline of her lip rouge,
our flashy appearance is our undoing and the authorities are

demanding that we disguise ourselves as birds, caught in our hideouts, to await the carts and cages that will transport us to the stadium, we talked, we talked endlessly about what species of bird we are going to choose as though what we were discussing was a costume for a masked ball, a tern with a black hood and a white throat, a forked tail, an erratic flight pattern? a ringdove with a gray rump, striped wings and a speckled neck?, a blackish starling, with a subtle green and purple iridescence?, a duck with a dangling crest, an orange mustache cover, a pale ring and stripe around its eyes, the inside of its wings blue with pale green reflections

crowded together on the little swings and around the drinking cups of the aviary where they have us on exhibition, we jabber like schoolgirls as we discuss our choice of costumes and fancy dress, combining the models and colors of the outfits in an irresistible urge to attain a delirious harmony, don't go to sleep on me, please, are you listening to me?

I was alone, she had vanished

serene, fleet of wing, inclined to fly to the heights, subtle, colorless, perfect, I plunged into profound contemplation of the virtues of the solitary bird in the meadow once again, grass, smell of cattle dung, copses of beech trees, murmuring streams nearby, little flowers, bees, sweet summertime solicitude, solar mildness, slight breeze, harmonious hills, soft tinkle of little bells, syncopated voices, faint barks, serene verdure of promenades lined with poplars and riverbank foliage

nothing allowed one to suspect the luminous apparition of those anointed contestants in a country wrestling match, the intense and exciting odor of their oiled bodies, lubricious pectorals and shoulder blades, spontaneous and self-confident smiles, rustic mustaches, deep, subtle, liquid eyes

was it a mere illusion brought on by the drug injected by the doctor? or were they projecting a video of the contests on the front wall of my room?

(why?)

(what for?)

did they want to put me to the test, as Ben Aïds had warned me, so as to discover my intimate preferences and include me in the band of those who were plague-ridden?, were they intending to revive my moribund senses so as to make me drain life in one last draft, before carrying out the probable sentence?, mirage, vision or Fata Morgana, the image was imposing and overwhelming, knotted vine shoots, solid arms, tendons, rough shorts, lengths of worn rope, opulently swollen, sagging crotches, the very image and likeness of robustness and ferocity, emblematic radiation

with their instruments of detection, did they record on my charts the sudden swift surge of my blood, abrupt heart palpitations, delight and nostalgia linked to that offering of friendship all too long in coming, welcoming bosoms, cordial faces, a look understanding my desires, that almost extinct and now impossible love?

quickly, swiftly, cling to the fleeting shadow of time, grab your desires by the tail, go back fervently over your most beautiful memories, store up images of bodies, faces, handsome members, happy moments, fulfilled longings, recall the blissful plenitude of your verses and your ardent reading of them aloud, not forgetting the smile and image of those who inspired you, the piano notes played expressly for you, your torments and pleasures as a person in love, hurry, there's no more time, the last grains of sand are trickling through the hourglass on the little night table, friars commissars sneaks stool-pigeons nurses doctors appear to be milling about the bed with gauze masks and protective gloves, it has all been as short, dense, passionate and confused as a dream, early years studies vocation writing ecstatic bliss, all dreamed!, persecutions imprisonment punishment burned manuscripts, nothing but a dream!, convent cell procession in cages solitude of love wounded in the dark roomettes, all of them a dream too! awaken penetrate to the very heart of the dream that contains your dream, the circle of formless material that surrounds and encompasses it, your life has been hard, are the streams of light that are dazzling you the fruit of hyperaesthesia?, of a new, stronger drug that your keepers have injected you with?, or have you at last reached the Lotus Terminal and its gently flowing rivers?, recite, recite yet again the verses translated by Ben Aïds, passion perseveres and union is long in coming, the meeting does not take place and one's patience grows exhausted, if love with you is an impossibility, promise that I may at least hope for it and prolong my hope even though it is not your intention to realize it, waiting for you without fulfillment is infinitely sweeter to me than the yes of a solicitous lover!

talk he said

was he the doctor? merely a jailer? perhaps the evil-tongued prior of the Unreformed Carmelites?, the Apostolic Nuncio in person?, some commissar or executioner under the orders of the enemy?

in the inner wine cellar of my Beloved I drank a wine that intoxicated us before the creation of the vineyard

deformed faces, protuberant, shapeless, grotesquely covered with prayer shawls and veils, piercing, rimless glasses with a disquieting gleam

drink it straight or mix it with the saliva of the Beloved, any other mixture would be sacrilege

they bent down toward him convinced that he was making confession, ready to absolve him in extremis of nonexistent heresies and crimes, the wine and saliva of the Beloved!, an idea daring and powerful, swift as a lightning flash of darkness amid the blinding light they were projecting, which mercilessly penetrated his eyelids, took possession of him, and left him trembling, might he not have contracted the illness along with them?, how to complain to the physician about the disease if the disease came from the Physician?, the boldness of the intuition took him by surprise and he repeated it under his breath to keep his spirits up

what is he saying?, is he unburdening his conscience?, no, he's reciting verses of the founder intermingled with those of Muslim sectarians, he is identifying himself in an impious way with the saint, he is raving, he is blaspheming, he is still in a state of delirium

if the illness that was doing him in and reducing him to a specter following the irruption of the Long-Legged one into their chapels and black chambers came from the spirits and saliva of the Beloved, the plague was a sacred gift, the punishment a benediction!, was not the one who had infected him in the desired garden of delight, his neck resting in the gentle arms of the Beloved, present in him in his very absence?,

was there not a tenderness in his extreme rigor? possessed of his
fatal gift, marked by his divine seal, could he not now enter a
place he knew not where and remain there not knowing
whether with or without a mainstay?, lights, blinding beams,
incandescence, soothing closeness to Her, a long hallway of the
run-down mansion that led to the piano and the melancholy
playing of the Sonata, free at last of the horde of his torturers
on the threshold of the solitary night, awaiting Naquir and
Muncar in the shadows of the underground chamber, pressures,
confined spaces, anxieties, interrogation, confrontation, subtle
vagabondage of his double or ka alongside the tomb of Ibn Al
Farid within the walls of the City of the Dead

VI

the Assembly of the Birds!

a restless and light bird, I gave a blind leap in the dark and, in some strange manner, I made a thousand flights in one to join my peers in the vast enclosure of that most splendid aviary equipped with perches, swings, drinking cups, trays, hanging flowerpots with twining creepers and tropical plants, jardinieres with ferns of exuberant luxuriance, pools of artificial stone, banks of finest sand

had I been invited intentionally?, was it a general convocation?, or, worse still, could I have fallen like the others, stupidly taken in by the whistle of a wily hunter

like that royal peacock which, having been hooded and placed in a basket for many long years, had lost amid the darkness and the indignity of its attire its consciousness and even the memory of its intrinsic beauty and the magnificence of the garden in which it found itself, and disturbed none the less by the fragrance of the flowers and the melodies of the birds, made despondent by desire and the nostalgia for a lost and forgotten reality suddenly broke through the veils enveloping it and emerged into the splendor of the garden and the iridescence of colors that adorned it, I was reborn to a serene and diaphanous life, endowed with a new and fresher appearance, joyously lost on purpose so as to be found again

was it a transmigration?

my wings, motor organs of support and propulsion in the air reinforced by adequate musculature, exquisite perfection of plumage and the invaluable aid of a tail possessed of a great diversity of stabilizing and directional functions, could aspire not only to agile leaps and glorious glides but also to the delights of controlled flight, the tenuous intoxication of weightless levitation

ever since my arrival in the antechamber of that paradise called chama, I had remained absorbed in contemplation and the learning of visual languages, ostentatious flights and adornments, display of showy colors and eccentricities of plumage,

while certain birds were dressed in dull yellow with humble
camouflage patterns others chose extravagant tails and crests,
the chromatic varieties of dress extended from intense copper
and orange-red to soft and delicate pastel colors, a little
orchestra of weavers was engaged in a flashy courtship dance,
furiously waving their fans to show them off and accompanying themselves with a faint hoarse song
who was I and what did I look like?
amid swings, tree trunks, lianas, branches and other play
equipment, I noted the existence of a tiny mirror and in one
brief flight planted myself before it
I recognized myself
contrasting with the abundance of plumed crests and the flutter
of flabella all about me, my sobriety, austerity and palest of
colors were those of the little bird described in the *Treatise*
I was immediately invaded by an intense and sweet satisfaction, I swayed gently back and forth on the swing and
enjoyed without the least boredom that fantastic congregation,
canaries with a soft, musical, versatile song, doves of exotic
and caricatural shapes, blackbirds with elongated tails and a
delicately modulated song, birds of sumptuous or modest
appearance with a mild trill and a lively warble, apathetic
grain-eaters with a gloomy introverted air, vivacious humming-
birds zooming round and round little bells, starlings of a
thoughtful and mischievous sort, energetic and active species,
the lovebird and its longed-for companion, fellow creatures
with dark eyes as though recently escaped from a conjurer's top
hat, specimens without feathers or subject to seasonal
mutations, gray cardinals, long-legged birds with cinnamon-
colored breasts, capuchin pigeons with black heads, all of them
arrayed in the vegetation and leafy shade of the aviary in
accordance with a scrupulous and subtle hierarchy
we remained on the lookout for telltale signs of a past existence
and, through short and uniform warbles, musical strophes with
varied pauses, sustained humming, songs of liquid cadence or a

mixture of sweet and rasping notes, we understood and identified each other

wasn't the parrot with the yellow tail that had two elongated green plumes running down the center of it one of the ladies comfortably settled on the terrace in the shell-shaped wicker armchairs, the parakeet with the washed-out overall coloration and a red rump the ancient Kirghiz in striped pajamas from the library?, the macaw with the strident voice and vainglorious acrobatics the prior of the Greek monastery, separated for once from his familiar?

in the chaffinch with the bright eyes and ocher superciliary stripe I thought I could make out the interrogative gaze of the older gentleman, in the sparrow with the black breast the silhouette of the daring young professor of Arabic

in what branches or thicket of the aviary was She?

freed from an illusory and sterile envelope, emerged from the oppressive hood and basket into the sweetness and newness of the garden, we had been reborn light and lithe, and in groups of thirty, as in the well known Persian text, we were readying ourselves for the arduous and exciting journey, the flight over the seven steep and rugged valleys to the solitary summit where S., the ethereal, colorless and ecstatic bird that is an allegory for the soul that has forsaken the world in the visions and raptures of the saint reigns

we listened, with deep spiritual absorption and fervor we listened

it begins the flight without ceasing to be immobile, travels without covering the slightest distance, draws closer and traverses no space whatsoever, all colors emanate from it but it has no color, it nests in the East without its place in the West remaining empty, the sciences proceed from its enchantment and the most perfect musical instruments from its echo and its resonances, it feeds on fire and whoever takes a feather

from its wings on its right side will emerge unharmed
from the flames, nature's breeze springs from its breath
and hence the lover reveals to it the heart's mysteries and
its most intimate and secret thoughts

but trills, melodies, warbles, modulations, coos, transmit
orders to depart, impatient rumors, movements of wings
drown out its voice, announce the beginning of the long march
all he had time for was to hurriedly copy his verses

> she lived in solitude
> and in solitude has made her nest
> and in solitude is guided
> by her beloved, alone as well
> in the solitude of wounded love

before flying with the other birds and closing once and for all
the pages of the book finally written

THE SPIRITUAL CANTICLE

by St John of the Cross

BRIDE

1. Where have You hidden,
Beloved, and left me moaning?
You fled like the stag
After wounding me;
I went out calling You, and
   You were gone.

2. Shepherds, you that go
Up through the sheepfolds to
   the hill,
If by chance you see
Him I love most,
Tell Him that I sicken, suffer,
and die.

3. Seeking my Love
I will head for the mountains
   and for watersides,
I will not gather flowers,
Nor fear wild beasts;
I will go beyond strong men
   and frontiers.

4. O woods and thickets
Planted by the hand of my
   Beloved!
O green meadow,
Coated, bright, with flowers,
Tell me, has He passed by you?

5. Pouring out a thousand
   graces,
He passed these groves in haste;
And having looked at them,
With His image alone,
Clothed them in beauty.

6. Ah, who has the power to
   heal me?
Now wholly surrender yourself!
Do not send me
Any more messengers,
They cannot tell me what I
   must hear.

7. All who are free
Tell me a thousand graceful
   things of You;
All wound me more
And leave me dying
Of, ah, I-don't-know-what
   behind their stammering.

8. How do you endure
O life, not living where you
   live?
And being brought near death
By the arrows you receive
From that which you conceive
   of your Beloved.

9. Why, since You wounded
This heart, don't You heal it?
And why, since You stole it
   from me,

Do You leave it so,
And fail to carry off what You
  have stolen?

10. Extinguish these miseries,
Since no one else can stamp
  them out;
And may my eyes behold You,
Because You are their light,
And I would open them to You
  alone.

11. O spring like crystal!
If only, on your silvered-over
  face,
You would suddenly form
The eyes I have desired,
Which I bear sketched deep
  within my heart.

12. Withdraw them, Beloved,
I am taking flight!

BRIDEGROOM

Return, dove,
The wounded stag
Is in sight on the hill,
Cooled by the breeze of your
  flight.

BRIDE

13. My Beloved is the
  mountains,
And lonely wooded valleys,
Strange islands,

And resounding rivers,
The whistling of love-stirring
  breezes,

14. The tranquil night
At the time of the rising dawn,
Silent music,
Sounding solitude,
The supper that refreshes, and
  deepens love.

15. Our bed is in flower,
Bound round with linking dens
  of lions,
Hung with purple,
Built up in peace,
And crowned with a thousand
  shields of gold.

16. Following Your footprints
Maidens run along the way;
The touch of a spark,
The spiced wine,
Cause flowings in them from
  the balsam of God.

17. In the inner wine cellar
I drank of my Beloved, and,
  when I went abroad
Through all this valley
I no longer knew anything,
And lost the herd which I was
  following.

18. There He gave me His
    breast;
There He taught me a sweet
    and living knowledge;
And I gave myself to Him,
Keeping nothing back;
There I promised to be His
    bride.

19. Now I occupy my soul
And all my energy in His
    service;
I no longer tend the herd,
Nor have I any other work
Now that my every act is love.

20. If, then, I am no longer
Seen or found on the common,
You will say that I am lost;
That, stricken by love,
I lost myself, and was found.

21. With flowers and emeralds
Chosen on cool mornings
We shall weave garlands
Flowering in Your love,
And bound with one hair of
    mine.

22. You considered
That one hair fluttering at my
    neck;
You gazed at it upon my neck
And it captivated You;
And one of my eyes wounded
    You.

23. When You looked at me
Your eyes imprinted Your grace
    in me;
For this You loved me ardently;
And thus my eyes deserved
To adore what they beheld in
    You.

24. Do not despise me;
For if, before, You found me
    dark,
Now truly You can look at me
Since You have looked
And left in me grace and
    beauty.

25. Catch us the foxes,
For our vineyard is now in
    flower,
While we fashion a cone of
    roses
Intricate as the pine's;
And let no one appear on the
    hill.

26. Be still, deadening north
    wind;
South wind come, you that
    waken love,
Breathe through my garden,
Let its fragrance flow,
And the Beloved will feed amid
    the flowers.

BRIDEGROOM

27. The bride has entered
The sweet garden of her desire,
And she rests in delight,
Laying her neck
On the gentle arms of her
  Beloved.

28. Beneath the apple tree:
There I took you for My own,
There I offered you My hand,
And restored you,
Where your mother was
  corrupted.

29. Swift-winged birds,
Lions, stags, and leaping roes,
Mountains, lowlands, and river
  banks,
Waters, winds, and ardors,
Watching fears of night:

30. By the pleasant lyres
And the siren's song, I conjure
  you
To cease your anger
And not touch the wall,
That the bride may sleep in
  deeper peace.

BRIDE

31. You girls of Judea,
While among flowers and roses
The amber spreads its perfume,

Stay away, there on the
  outskirts:
Do not so much as seek to
  touch our thresholds.

32. Hide Yourself, my Love;
Turn Your face toward the
  mountains,
And do not speak;
But look at those companions
Going with her through strange
  islands.

BRIDEGROOM

33. The small white dove
Has returned to the ark with an
  olive branch;
And now the turtledove
Has found its longed-for mate
By the green river banks.

34. She lived in solitude,
And now in solitude has built
  her nest;
And in solitude He guides her,
He alone, who also bears
In solitude the wound of love.

BRIDE

35. Let us rejoice, Beloved,
And let us go forth to behold
  ourselves in Your beauty,
To the mountain and to the
  hill,
To where the pure water flows,

And further, deep into the
    thicket.

36. And then we will go on
To the high caverns in the rock
Which are so well concealed;
There we shall enter
And taste the fresh juice of the
    pomegranates.

37. There You will show me
What my soul has been seeking,
And then You will give me,
You, my Life, will give me
    there
What You gave me on that
    other day:

38. The breathing of the air,
The song of the sweet
    nightingale,
The grove and its living beauty
In the serene night,
With a flame that is consuming
    and painless.

39. No one looked at her,
Nor did Aminadab appear;
The siege was still;
And the cavalry,
At the sight of the waters,
    descended.

ACKNOWLEDGMENTS

To Luce López Baralt, José Angel Valente and José Martín Arancibia, without whose encouragement, empathy and aid I would not have been able to carry out my undertaking; to Monique Lange, for her active presence in my creative "emptiness"; to Abdelhadi; to Jorge Ronet, *in memoriam*; to Marcel Bataillon (*Erasmus and Spain*), José María Blanco White (*Observations on Heresy and Orthodoxy*), Francisco Delicado (*Retrato de la lozana andaluza*), Emile Dermenghem (*Essai sur la mystique musulmane*, prologue to Ibn Al Farid's *Al Jamriya*), Al Attar (*The Language of the Birds*), Luis de Góngora (*Solitudes*), Crisógeno de Jesús (*Vida de San Juan de la Cruz*) Mawlana (*Odes to Chams Tabrizi*), Marcelino Menéndez Pelayo (*Historia de los heterodoxos españoles*), Angela Selke (*El Santo Oficio de la Inquisición*), Leszek Kolakowski (*Christians without a Church*), Luce López Baralt (*San Juan de la Cruz y el Islam*), Suhravardi (*Three Treatises on Mysticism*), Colin Peter Thompson (*The Poet and the Mystic, A study of the "Cántico Espiritual" of San Juan de la Cruz*), whose works I refer to or cite in various passages of the book. To San Juan de la Cruz, whose *Obra Completa* (Licino Ruano de la Iglesia edition) forms the vertebral structure of the novel.